SHUDDER

By
Ashley McCook

ISBN: 978-09571255-3-7

Also by Ashley McCook

DEMON'S DAUGHTER
(The Emily Trilogy, Book 1)

DEMON'S REVENGE
(The Emily Trilogy, Book 2)

DEMON'S BLOOD
(The Emily Trilogy, Book 3)

Crooked Halo Publications

www.ashleymccook.co.uk

SHUDDER

By
Ashley McCook

Published by

Crooked Halo Publications

www.ashleymccook.co.uk

This is a work of fiction. Names, characters, places and incidents are either products of the author's imagination or are used fictitiously. Any resemblance to actual events or locales or persons, living or dead, save those clearly in the public domain, is purely coincidental.

Shudder © 2013 Ashley McCook

ISBN: 978-09571255-3-7

All rights reserved. No part of this work may be reproduced or transmitted in any form buy any electronic or mechanical means, including photocopying, recording, or by any information storage and retrieval system, without the prior written permission of the publisher, except for short quotes used for review or promotion. For information address the publisher.

Graphic Design by Nigel Johnston

For Mum and Dad
Love you xx

Prologue

As usual there were eight of them.

Frank stood near the middle of the room, his hip against a moulding chair that looked as though it might have come off the Ark. He checked his watch for maybe the hundredth time. It was finally midnight. He sighed and looked around him. The only light in the room came from a small kerosene lamp which was hissing hysterically as it tried to illuminate the dark corners. He assumed the tech guys enjoyed fooling with them – surely the intelligence community, if that's who ran these ops, had more high spec equipment than a damn kerosene lamp? The others in the group leaned against the walls, sat on one of the dusty chairs or stood sentry just inside the windows staring out into the unending darkness.

He knew that all of them would have been hand-picked, the elite, top of their field, trained to kill. And here they waited in the near dark, miles away from anything, ready for action, armed to the teeth; and wearing Halloween masks.

It looked bizarre – combats and heavy army-issue boots topped by various witches, ghouls, devils and the freaky white one from the 'Scream' movie. Frank was a green witch. He sighed again. The heavy latex was making him sweat and the witch hair was tickling his neck. A ghoul by the window asked for a cigarette. Several witches patted down inside pockets and came up with a box of Marlborough and a red lighter. Frank could see the name of a bar stencilled onto the side. He looked away fast. It was one of their orders – no-one makes any buddies and no-one gets into a position where he can ID one of the others. Knowing too much could cost you your job. Or worse.

He found himself thinking that it could be the same eight every time. Being well trained had its downside when you were able to recognise voice patterns and accents no matter what kind of mask was being worn and no matter how clear your orders had been. He wondered if SHE knew; if his voice was as familiar to her as hers had become to him. The idea made him shiver.

The ghoul headed into what was left of the bathroom and lit

1

up, the hiss and click of the lighter unnaturally loud in the silence. Ghoul man inhaled deeply and sighed contentedly. Frank checked his watch again.

"We keeping you from something, soldier?" asked the scream guy.

Frank looked at him for a moment. "As a matter of fact, Angelina Jolie's waiting for me in one of the other rooms."

"In this place?" A purple devil gestured around the filth.

"Sure. Angie likes a little mess with her rough and tumble," Frank grinned under his mask. The others chuckled softly.

Frank checked out their surroundings to keep his mind away from the direction his thoughts had been heading. This must have been a decent hotel once, just built in the wrong location, for a city that had died before it had even become a town. The carpet was a deep blue, with swirls of green and red. The walls might once have been a light grey, wall lights trailing cobwebs were still in place near where the bed would have been and there was even a main lamp over near the desk. The bed was long gone, ingrained marks on the wall showed where it had been until the vandals or looters had their way with it. The desk had been bolted down and it remained against the inside wall, thick with dust and mouse droppings. The chairs were standard hotel issue, lumpy and uncomfortable. Frank couldn't see why they'd been left here. Or perhaps they'd been moved in yesterday, once the rendezvous point had been decided.

A low whistle sounded from just outside the door - the signal that someone was coming. The men in the room fanned out immediately, checked their radios and then stood ready. No more leaning against the walls or inhaling borrowed smokes. Frank stood up and checked his radio with a soft "S19", their code for the night. There was an answering burst of static and command whispered "Received" into his earpiece. So far so good. Frank checked his weapon and took the safety off.

A car came slowly up the long drive towards the hotel. "Standby S19" control was saying. The full beam from the car lights pieced the gloom of the little room and Frank winced at the brightness. Sweat trickled down his back and he shifted as it tickled him.

The car stopped, the lights went out and a car door opened, then closed. The gravel crunched as the occupant of the car walked slowly towards the doorway and stopped. Frank could see the shadow on the stoop. He took a breath as control told him to "Proceed".

"Confirm," he said in a loud voice.

"S19" was the answer and Frank spoke to his radio, "Confirmed." He stood back and the woman stepped into the room. She was wearing plain blue jeans and a black t-shirt with "Save the drama for your Mama" stencilled on it, along with an old crone witch mask. The hair on the mask was long and purple. She studied them all for a moment.

"I feel stupid," she said.

Frank laughed. "You were Bill Clinton last time."

"Yeah, but I didn't have a wart the size of Boston on the side of my nose."

"Or purple hair," Frank pointed towards the table and grinned as she tsked in disgust.

"Housekeeping is shabby. Let's not stay here again," she told him, pulling over a chair. Her voice was husky and mellow with an American accent dulled by the rhythm of another – English maybe? – Frank pretended once again not to notice and motioned to Ghoul man who moved forward, spreading a large piece of plastic over the table. The woman looked up at him. "Better," she said.

Another agent stepped up and put a heavy briefcase on the table. Scream guy moved to her right and produced a key. He opened the case and they both stepped back out of the way. They were all wearing latex gloves.

"Perimeter," Frank spoke into his radio again. Two of the men in the room moved outside and he could hear exchanges from the others stationed around the perimeter.

The woman sighed. She sat looking at the briefcase for a few moments and then leaned forward and opened it. Frank stood on the left of the table, facing her. No matter how many times he watched this, the chill that slid down his spine when she worked never faded. He felt it now as she removed the evidence bag from the case. She shook it and it unrolled. Inside was a toothbrush, totally unremarkable in its ordinariness, a blue toothbrush with white bristles. The woman studied it from all angles and then reached into the case again, removing a pair of scissors. She slit the top of the bag quickly and took the brush out; holding it carefully like it was made of porcelain. She never wore gloves. Closing her hands around the toothbrush she began to speak. Frank had a notebook ready.

He was good with shorthand.

****

Harry Grogan sat down at the counter and ordered a coffee with the special. He looked around. It was a small town with a small diner and most of the sparse patrons looked older than God. None of them looked like feds, or mob lackeys.

Harry gulped down his coffee before the pancakes arrived and got a refill from the waitress along with a big smile. He grinned back feeling relaxed. He'd been on the run for almost six weeks, although he was starting to wonder who exactly he was running from. If he was such a big deal then surely someone would've found him by now. Maybe he was too good for them all.

The problem was that he had information: Lots of it. Information linking Anthony Boccanegra, Cesar Delfino and Walter Pescetti with organized crime throughout Washington. He'd worked for all three of their houses for almost forty years and when the feds had approached him, he'd jumped ship with no qualms at all. His money was safe and they could give him a new identity to enjoy it. And then his family started disappearing – his brothers first, then his sister, his wife. He received a photograph of his daughter, Chloe, taken outside her school, and he snapped.

Escaping from the feds had been easy; killing the two who'd been assigned to protect him had been disagreeable but necessary. And so here he was, living off the money he'd cleaned out of his accounts during the past two years – no-one misses money when it walks out little by little – and keeping his head down by moving from place to place and staying off the pay-rolls and the police and busy body radars.

The pancakes were good, served with syrup. A great stack of them, hot from the griddle. He thought about Chloe, wondered for the thousandth time how his baby was and then pushed her from his mind. Looking back was going to get him caught, and getting caught was going to get her dead.

Harry shovelled the last piece of pancake into his mouth and grinned in satisfaction. It wasn't a bad life.

The feeling came over him all of a sudden – the hairs on the back of his neck stood to attention and fear roiled in his gut. Harry looked around. Someone was watching him. That's what all of his senses were screaming at him. His eyes darted around checking it all out. The diner's patrons were more interested in their food or the morning paper; the two cars parked outside were empty. No-one lingered on the sidewalks. There was nothing. But the feeling wouldn't leave him.

And then his heart almost stopped. For just a moment it had felt as though a cold hand had pressed onto the hot skin at the nape of his neck.

Harry shuddered.

****

In the dirty ruins of the Southern Belle Hotel, the woman sat back from the table. She had been sitting there for almost an hour. Her voice had grown more and more tired, and Frank had been close to kneeling down beside her, taking her hand and asking if she'd like a rest. That would've been a serious breach of protocol and probably the end of his involvement in this project. He'd managed to resist the temptation.

"Did you get all that?" she asked, sounding shaky.

Frank nodded and flipping back the pages of the notebook, spoke into his radio. "S19. Main information following. He's in Kentucky, a small town called Redbrook, staying at the "Four Paces" guest house. He pays in cash. He's dyed his hair brown, has plenty of money to keep going and intends to make for his brother's summer place in Maine. There's no record of it in any of their books – it's a retreat." He paused and received a confirmation from control. He knew that a team was in place already and would be underway within ten or fifteen minutes. Their job was done. He motioned to the others who began to pack away the suitcase and all traces of their visit. The woman mumbled something and

Frank leaned in to listen.

"He's eating pancakes with syrup." she whispered, turning exhausted grey eyes to him. "And he worries about his daughter."

Frank felt that chill again. He straightened up, longing suddenly for his warm bed and the simple pleasure of curling up beside his wife. He thought he should ask if the woman would be okay driving to wherever she was supposed to go but he knew it was against the rules. Get there, get the info, and get out. It was a simple mission every time. He backed away from her and out of the door, walking swiftly away without looking back.

****

Chapter One

It was a perfect night to run. The whole beach was bathed in moonlight, sea grasses waving gently in the off-shore breeze, the sand restored to smooth perfection by the outgoing tide. She ran up the shore and back, three miles in all, enjoying the wind in her hair and the sharp taste of salt on her lips. It helped to have Bruce Springsteen blasting into her brain and she cranked up the volume on her ever present iPod as "Thunder Road" began. Running was simple – one foot in front of the other, keep the rhythm going, feel the burn in your muscles, work past the pain. Her mind focused on the task and the steady beat of her feet on the ground and the music in her ears.

At the bottom of the set of steep steps which led off the strand and onto the walk back to town, she paused and looked back. Her footprints stretched back behind her and she knew that the pull of the next tide would erase them again. It would be just as 'though she'd never been there. She shook herself and set off again.

Back along the cliff walk she sang along to the rest of the "Greatest Hits" album, uncaring if she was out of tune. At 2:30 in the morning there wouldn't be anyone around to hear anyway. At the last corner before home she stopped, panting, hands on hips, then checked her stopwatch. Not bad. A whole three seconds faster than the last time. She clasped her hands and stretched them out above her head then shook out each leg in turn. From here she'd walk and cool down.

As she rounded the corner, the bay came into view and she caught her breath, moved by its beauty as much now as the first day she'd seen it. The pure silver moon glittering on the ink black sea, the far off crash of waves onto rocks at the mouth of the harbour, the muted glow of streetlights in the otherwise dark town beyond. Home. She smiled broadly.

Her natural wariness reasserted itself as she reached the top of the last set of steps that led onto the crescent below. Sliding into the shadows of the cliff, she looked over the scene before her.

On the east side of the bay was a small harbour with a row of four large town houses standing guard behind it. There was only room for three small fishing boats and the Pilot boat which was called upon several times a day to aid larger vessels navigating the dangerous stretch of coast. From the harbour, running west was the promenade, with two lanes of traffic and a collection of shops and guest houses. The shops were typical of a sea-side resort – several clothes shops, shoe shop, newsagent, café, bakery and a well-known ice-cream parlour.

Her eyes swung along the line of shops to the children's playground. The moon cast a silver glow into the shadows. It looked unearthly, eerie and yet she knew that in the light of day it was just a collection of swings and climbing frames painted in bright primary colours. She'd been here for twelve years now – a sizeable chunk of her thirty-two years on the planet. The people were warm and welcoming, no-one asked a lot of personal questions (a by-product of the troubles and the recent peace, Mitch had told her) although she suspected that many of them had made up a plethora of interesting stories about who she was and where she came from. She looked down on this scene so often from here on the cliff walk, from her own veranda, from the café or the ice-cream parlour that it was forever imprinted in her mind's eye. She recalled it all the time in her dreams and on those occasions when work took her away. Her own slice of heaven - a peaceful haven from reality.

Content that the town was safe and nothing lurked in the darkness other than sleepy sea-birds and the odd mouse, she started down the steps towards her home. Bruce was singing about the pain of unrequited desire and she hummed along.

"Great song," she told the cliff, patting the rock as she went past.

'Rock Haven' was once a smugglers cottage, built (as the name suggested) on the rock at the base of the cliff. From the cellar you could access at least three underground passages which led down to a small cave and out into the bay. The romance and history of the place delighted her, especially when Mitch had recounted the local legend of the 'Grey Lady Ghost'.

"What ghost?" She'd asked, hopping up onto the counter beside him.

He'd smiled, blue eyes twinkling. "Sure you won't be scared?" She'd rolled her eyes. "…Ok then. There was this nun, right?"

"From the Dominican."

"Yep. On top of the cliff, when it was still an abbey and not just a school. Well, this nun, she fell in love with one of the smugglers. He was on the run from the law and she'd met him during one of her walks around the bay at low tide. A right jack the lad he was, but she tobered him…"

"Tobered?"

"Um…tamed, if you like. He fell in love right back and they used to meet secretly for a bit of…y'know…shenanigans."

He'd thrown her that look of his, the 'Mitch Special' she called it, the one that heralded the start of his flirting routine. She'd giggled and swatted him.

"Anyway…the Mother Superior found out and told this nun that she'd have to leave. Obviously. But somehow this girl persuaded her Mother Superior that she'd finish it and return to God or something. Whatever she promised, the old Mother let her stay on. But she obviously didn't trust the girl that much 'cause she told the law and they were watching the nun the next time she went to meet him."

"Oh shit," She was wide eyed.

"Aye deed. There was a big fight and the smuggler was killed. The nun of course saw the whole thing. I suppose the Mother Superior maybe thought it would teach her a lesson or perhaps that she was removing the source of the nun's temptation and she'd be a good girl from then on but it wasn't meant to be."

"No?"

"No. See the Mother hadn't reckoned on the power of it."

"The power of what? God?"

"Not at all. The power of love. Huey Lewis got that song right. The nun decided that she didn't want to live without her lover and, full of guilt for having led the law to him, she climbed to the top of the cliff and threw herself off, just above his little cottage

– our house now. Some people who stayed in the place before you bought it were convinced that they heard someone walking around late at night calling out. It was her damned soul, looking for him. Even in death she wanted to be with him."

She had looked wistfully around the house. "Wow. How romantic is that?!"

"What? Jumping off a cliff? Are all you yanks this sad?" Mitch had snorted and gone back to chopping carrots for his speciality dish – Irish stew. Shannon had felt, in the way only eighteen year olds can, the excitement of having a tragic love story come alive all around her.

Looking at the house now, she was glad that she'd spent all the money on it. It was her dream home, her special place. The one place she felt that she could relax and be herself. Even now, in the depths of the night, it felt peaceful and secure. She walked slowly up the short driveway with its majestic weeping willow and past the small garden with its path of crushed shells which was still a work in progress. From here the house was all angular and seemed haphazard. The door was green with a small pane of glass surrounded by stained glass inlays. There was a picture window above the door etched with the scene of a ship out in the bay.

She switched off the iPod and went inside, closing the door quietly behind her, and stood in the hall for a moment, letting the stillness of the sleeping house envelop her.

The ground floor was the functional part of the house – kitchen with breakfast nook and utility, garage, office and two small guest bedrooms. A spiral staircase from the kitchen led upstairs into a small, formal dining room whilst another set of stairs close to the front door led to a landing which accessed the other bedrooms and the main living area.

The back of the house was all glass to maximize the incredible views over the bay and the ocean and a wooden veranda wrapped itself around the upper floor right from the master bedroom to the corner of the living room. A small part of the veranda jutted out over the top of the utility room downstairs. Standing there felt like you were surrounded by the sea and she never tired of it.

Mitch was asleep, or pretending to be. She could hear him snoring softly. Taking a glass of wine from the kitchen, she headed upstairs, opened the French doors from her bedroom and sat down on one of the loungers. From here the sea looked like black glass, stained with silver where the moon touched it. She sipped her wine, closed her eyes and felt the day's stress fall from her shoulders.

The wine was a good Australian chardonnay. She downed the glass too fast and smiled at the sudden fuzziness in her head. A seagull cried somewhere on the hill above the harbour, and was answered by a dog in the town. She thought about getting another glass of wine, stood up and walked towards the rail to look out over the town of dark houses. She wondered about the people there. What were they dreaming about? Was no-one else awake? It was unusual for her to feel afraid and yet it seemed as though her senses were constantly on alert these days, as though her body was aware of some present danger before her brain had fully accepted it.

A movement in the harbour car-park caught her eye. She strained to see more clearly. For almost a minute there was nothing. She remained absolutely still, her heart thudding in her chest. Then it happened again – a small light bloomed for a second in the darkness and was swallowed up again. She frowned in concentration. Was that a cigarette? She took a deep breath, exhaled and closed her eyes for a second. Then she went back inside and made her way to Mitch's room. She stood over him for a second, watching his chest rise and fall. For a moment her fists clenched at her sides and her mouth tightened. It passed. She schooled her face into a neutral expression and shook him awake.

He sat up in bed looking at her groggily and she thought for the thousandth time what a good looking man he was and how things could've been different between them.

"Time to wake up, gorgeous," she whispered.

"What is it?" he was suddenly awake, all his attention on her.

"We may be having a visitor soon. We should be ready."

Mitch didn't argue. He just got up and, with no attempt at

modesty, pulled on his t-shirt and boxer shorts, grinning at her over his shoulder. Shannon rolled her eyes. Ever the showman!

She went back out onto the veranda and watched the shadows of the harbour.

Chapter Two

He'd been watching when she rounded the cliff walk and made her way back to the house. Drinking almost cold coffee from a plastic cup and downing another two Advil to combat the headache. He'd taken too long to get here. The old man had told him that he had ten days at the most and that limit had passed yesterday. It had taken a lot of called in favours to get out of the States and even more good luck to make it here. He rubbed the stubble on his chin. He couldn't remember when he'd last eaten or slept properly. Never mind the last time he'd washed or changed his clothes. Strange then that what he wanted more than anything was a straight shot of vodka and a nice red pill embossed with a 'D'.

He rummaged in his pocket and found his last cigarette. He lit it and checked his watch, inhaling deeply into his lungs until he coughed around the smoke. Time was marching on; he'd need to make a move soon. The message had to be delivered now. Tonight. So far everything else the old man had told him was correct – she was reclusive, came out at night to go running, lived in a big house which looked as though it'd been cut out of the cliff face, lived with Mitch Connor and, well, this was the unproven bit, someone high up wanted her dead.

He got out of the car and leaned against the bonnet to finish the cigarette. He inhaled greedily again and looked towards the house. The approach would be everything and it had been so long since he had done anything like this. He could feel the shake in his hands, the tickling, crawling sensation on his skin. He knew his body was crying out for more…more booze, more pills…but he couldn't do anything about it. He'd made a promise and a life was at stake. A few more hours and then he'd find a nice Irish pub and drink himself back into the oblivion that the old man had dragged him out of fourteen days ago. Only fourteen days? Christ. He finished the cigarette and boosted himself off the bonnet. The sudden exertion produced a spasm of coughing. He waited until it passed and then headed for the house. Just deliver the message and then he'd be free.

He walked swiftly from the car park, staying in the shadows. He thought about the old man as he walked, the look of disgust on his face when he'd broken into the apartment and seen the state of his son. He was as tough as he'd ever been, age was catching up but he was still an impressive looking man. Almost 6'3" with broad shoulders and muscular arms, he had always seemed larger than life. Captain America with an FBI badge and a sharp suit, Ray bans and a Rolex. It was hardly surprising that his son had always been a disappointment, striving to match his famous father and never succeeding. Not surprising that his son had dropped out and spun further and further out of control when he'd found it impossible to even keep his family…he stopped and leaned against the lower promenade wall, breathing deep and willing away the mental pain as well as the physical.

It had been almost six years since he had spoken to his father, never mind been in the same room, so seeing the old man standing there in his squalid living room at six in the morning had been more than a shock. And why was he there? To give orders as usual, expecting his eldest son to obey without question, to honour his obligations to his father and his country, to travel halfway across the world to play knight in shining armour to some spoiled heiress with a price on her head and a secret that more than one agency seemed willing to kill for.

He shook his head. He still felt as though he was in the grip of the worst hangover in creation. His stomach clenched in pain. The drugs that had lived in his system for so long weren't leaving without a fight. He swayed against the wall and used both hands, bracing behind his back, to steady himself. He should never have agreed to do this. He should have kicked the old man out, poured another drink, popped another pill and prayed that this would be the shot that took him to hell. In six years he'd never even come close to the death that he longed for, just lived in a strange half-twilight place where images came and went along with the alcohol and the dealers. And when the time had finally come to face off with his father? Breeding had won over reason and here he was.

He pushed himself upright again and moved closer to the house. His father's gun was a welcome weight in the ill-fitting shoulder holster. The knife in his boot, even better, although he knew deep down that if he encountered any resistance here he was in no shape to defend himself. What a mess. Thanks Dad!

He moved through the garden as quickly as he could and into the shelter of the front door. The night had become quiet, or perhaps all sounds were drowned out by the impossibly loud beating of his heart. He paused. Forced entry or stealth was impossible. He would need to have his wits about him for either of those activities and for now his brain was too clouded. He considered and winced. If dear old Dad could see him now. He rang the doorbell.

The door opened almost immediately and he knew they had been waiting for him. Mitch Connor stood in front of him, as commanding a presence as his father and almost twenty years younger. He saw the surprise on Mitch's face, saw his lips moving but his heart was pounding even harder now and drowning out everything else. Reality slid sickeningly and he resisted the urge to vomit.

The message. He had to deliver it.

"Get her out," he growled. "Now." Then he fell forward into an internal darkness that for a blessed few minutes took away the pain in his head and his soul. His final thoughts, as the tiled hallway rose up to meet him, were of his father and how disappointed he would be. Again.

Chapter Three

Mitch dragged the unconscious figure further into the hall, turned him over and began searching through his pockets. He pulled out a wallet and opened it, rifling through receipts and a few dollars. He paused at a photograph, sighed and continued his search.

Shannon had been hiding behind the door. She closed it and stood watching as Mitch unearthed a knife from the slumped form's left ankle and a 9mm semi-automatic from a shoulder holster. He looked up at her wordlessly and carried the weapons off towards the kitchen.

Shannon moved a little closer to their visitor, tilting her head to study the man lying in her hall. He was, she thought, a little under six feet tall with broad shoulders and narrow hips. He was also filthy; his sandy hair was too long and lying in greasy tendrils. He had at least five days' growth of beard and he was pale with a slightly bloated look to his face and a crusted-over cut above his left eye. He was wearing what had once been dark blue jeans, a black shirt and a mid-length tan jacket. All the clothes were crumpled as though he'd been sleeping in them and the jacket had been torn and roughly patched in several places. She knelt down beside him and wrinkled her nose. He was badly in need of a shower although she was certain that was the least of his concerns – there was such a heavy, sickly aura around him that seemed to cling to his skin and contaminate the air in the hall.

Shannon reached out gingerly, pushed some of the slick hair off his forehead and placed her palm down. He was hot, feverish. Sweat was beading his skin and dripping into his stubble. She was about to call Mitch when the man's eyes opened and he sucked in a lungful of air with a twisting of his features. He was in pain, his chocolate brown eyes looked at her in anguish and he opened his mouth to speak. She hushed him, pushing him back as he struggled to get up.

"…message…," he mumbled.

"Don't try to speak," Shannon told him as he pulled himself up from under her hands. "You need to rest," she went on, trying to push him down again.

He shook his head and, mustering all his strength, finally managed to pull himself into a sitting position. His head was pounding again, his skin felt hot and he still needed to vomit. He closed his eyes, took a shuddering breath and wiped his forehead with his arm. He looked at the young woman sitting beside him and tried to keep himself from passing out again.

"I have a message for you," he croaked.

"You don't know me," she told him, frowning.

"Shannon," he said and began to cough, his body aching. Her brow creased with concern and Shannon reached an arm around his shoulders, supporting him until the spasm had passed. He looked up her. "You are, aren't you?"

Shannon nodded. The man looked around, for Mitch she assumed.

"He's in the kitchen, through there. He can't hear us."

He nodded once, glad she understood. This part was for her, and only her. His father had been adamant about that. "The message is…"

"From who?" she asked, suddenly she was even more attentive, her eyes glittering.

"Not important…" he said, "The message is that you have to leave here now. Tonight. Things have…gotten out of control. If you're here when they arrive then he can do nothing. I only had ten days to warn you and I took too long. Get moving." He pushed her but he was weak and the gesture was largely ineffective. He slid back to the floor, her supporting arm guiding him there carefully. His breath was ragged and his face crumpled as a lance of pain burst through his head.

"Mitch!" Shannon called, pressing two fingers to the side of his neck and checking his pulse. It was there but unsteady. His eyes opened again, looking at her for a few seconds before closing. Shannon struggled to pull him into a position where she could give him mouth to mouth if it became necessary. His jacket was heavy and seemed to have a mind of its own as she fought to move him. One side was trapped under his body and she yanked at it to free him. There was a heavy weight in the pocket and she felt the edges of it in case it was a weapon. It was rectangular and bulky so she opened the pocket and peeked in. Just a cell phone. She was about to reach in and lift it out when the man in the jacket rolled out of her grasp again, moaning.

"Mitch!" she called again, where the hell was he?

His eyelids opened again and his gaze slid over her, his eyeballs rolling back in his head. Shannon leaned over him, her fingers tracking his pulse. Her heart was thumping in fear. He moaned and she patted his face with her other hand.

"Stay with me, mister. I think I need you to get me out of this. Stay with me." She slapped a little harder, "Don't you check out on me, pal." He moaned again. "Dammit!" she gasped. "Mitch!!" her voice sounded frantic now.

And suddenly Mitch was beside her, a syringe in his hand. He had pulled on a jacket.

"Lay still, Matt. I'm going to give you something for the pain and the fever," he pulled Matt's sleeve up, yanked the end from the syringe with his teeth, spat it onto the floor and injected the contents.

Matt winced and looked up. His mouth wouldn't seem to work properly. He focused. "Leave me be, Mitch. It's been a shitty day," he managed to slur.

"Yeah, yeah. Nighty night, Matt," Mitch said, pulling his sleeve back down and throwing the syringe into the far corner of the hall. Matt had already passed out again.

Shannon turned her attention to Mitch, her expression carefully blank. "You know him?" she asked.

Mitch nodded. "Yeah, I know him. Seems like you still have friends in high places, Shan. What say we think about that later? Apparently we need to move out. He wasn't sent here in that state for fun. Let's go." He stood up and held his hand out to pull her up beside him. Shannon grasped it and nodded towards Matt.

"He has to come with us." she told him.

Mitch frowned. "He'll slow us down. He's a drunk and a drug

addict. He's been trying to do himself in for years. We should leave him."

Shannon chewed on her lip. She looked down at Matt. "Someone sent him," she began, "He's our only link to them. Without him, we're on our own."

Mitch looked at her. "I have friends," he said, "Places we can go. We're not on our own."

Shannon felt her heart skip a beat. She looked levelly back at Mitch. Their eyes locked, Mitch's suspicious, and Shannon's giving nothing away. "He comes with us," she said and walked away.

Mitch stood for a moment watching her back, his face expressionless, and then he moved to Matt's inert figure and dragged him to his feet. Time to move. They could argue later.

Chapter Four

The movement of the car jolted Matt Carter awake. He was lying across the back seat, loosely strapped in. He tried to move but his arms and legs felt like lead and only his head obeyed, the slightest inclination of his head sending fresh bolts of pain through his skull and he couldn't bite back the moan of pain.

"Hang in there, Matt. Another fifteen minutes and we'll be there." The voice came from the driver. Matt took a deep breath and twisted his head to get a better view. Pain tore through him again and he gave up, dropping his head back down onto the seat. He was breathing hard.

"He needs medical attention, Mitch. I don't think we can deal with this alone." The woman's voice was soft, slightly husky, as though she'd just woken up. Matt struggled to remember her, to gauge where he was and what was going on. There was a rustling of paper.

"Well, it was your idea to bring him so I hope you know some generous, discrete GP around here," Mitch's sarcasm was shot through with bitterness. "What are you reading in that rag anyway?"

"Huh? Oh, nothing really. That big mafia trial is on again."

"Yeah? They found the mole then?" Mitch whistled under his breath. "That guy was lucky it was just the feds who caught him. If the big three had found him first, he'd be fish bait."

'Er, yeah. I guess so," The paper rustled again and a shadow moved between Matt and the window. "How much further, Mitch? He really doesn't look so good."

Mitch sighed theatrically. "Like I said, another fifteen minutes and then you can get him inside and play doctors and nurses with him." The shadow moved away and daylight flashed across Matt's eyelids.

Matt frowned and slipped back into unconsciousness.

****

When he next woke, he was in a dimly lit room with a duvet tucked under his chin and a drip in his arm. He turned his head gingerly. There was a small charge of pain but none of the thunderbolts from before. He chanced turning his head a little further to look around the room. It wasn't worth the effort.

He supposed the place could be called functional – all it consisted of was his bed, a battered wardrobe and a small bedside cabinet. The walls seemed to have some ancient yellowing wallpaper on them. In fact, everything seemed tinged with sepia.

The door directly opposite the foot of the bed opened and Mitch came in. "Glad to see you awake, Matt," he said cheerfully but his smile didn't quite reach his eyes.

"Where…?" Matt managed to croak before a hacking cough took over. Mitch reached over him to the table and lifted a glass then helped him to drink a small amount of water through a straw. He took it away after a few seconds.

"Not too much at once, okay? We're at a safe house. You've been out for about three days and the Doc's been coming in every evening to check up on you." He paused and eyed Matt for a moment. "Gotta ask pal."

Matt nodded.

"Why'd he send you? I mean…" he gestured at the bed, "…look at you. How long has it been since you were running ops like this? How long since you stopped with the booze and the pills?"

Matt sighed. "What date is this?" he asked reaching up to rub his eyes with the heel of his hand.

"Huh? 22nd. Why?"

"Then I quit 18 days ago," Matt managed a wan smile. "Not my own choice."

"Lewis found you? Jesus…and you just did it? Hopped on a plane at his say so?" Mitch looked incredulous. He sat down on the edge of the bed. "He snaps his fingers and you jump. Man, what airline did he bribe to fly you out?"

Matt shook his head and Mitch frowned. "No, you couldn't take a commercial flight? And obviously he couldn't be seen to have anything to do with it? You go cross country and then …" he paused, thinking furiously. He clapped his hands, making Matt jump. "You went to De Franco and caught the Phantom. Where was the drop?"

"France and then over land to the ports. Big old cargo ship to Dublin." Matt grinned at Mitch.

"Dublin?" Mitch pretended to look around the room as his brain worked out the details. "You got the car from my Sean, switched the plates over the border. Just like you, Carter, all planned on the fly." He laughed softly and then swiftly lifted his head. "And someone was coming for us?" He focused on Matt again, his eyes fixed on his face.

Matt took his time. He could feel the hairs stand up on the back of his neck – it'd been a long time since he'd felt that. It had once been a joke among the men in his unit – they'd called it his "early warning system". Looking across the room at Mitch now was like looking into the night during a mission in Iraq. Every nerve ending he possessed was warning him that the man he had once thought of as a brother was a danger to him. Matt concentrated on breathing – taking air into his lungs, releasing it.

"Look, man, I was out of it. Dad came and asked me to take this on. I did it. I didn't think beyond that. All I know is that the old man still has his nose in a few intelligence files and he always had a soft spot for Shannon. He found out about the strike and sent me to warn you both." And for some reason he doesn't trust you, Matt thought to himself.

Mitch nodded slowly as he studied Matt. "So, who's your old man working for now?" he asked finally.

Matt grinned and leaned back on the pillows. "He's been retired for about four years. Well, officially anyway. I wasn't really in much of a state to think about it on the day he came to see me," he grinned, "I've had the odd spare moment in the past two weeks to think a bit. I mean, I'd like to think that he's just being a good Samaritan and helping out a friend in need but we both know that's not his bag. I mean, if it was something official then why didn't they send an agent? Even if this is Lewis Carter playing rogue, he could still have used one of the underground groups –

they still have enough respect for him to carry out orders with few questions." Matt watched Mitch under his lashes but his former colleague was giving nothing away.

"And you?" asked Mitch. "What are you doing here?"

Matt laughed softly. "Honestly, I have no idea. A misguided sense of loyalty? Guilt? A last chance to prove myself to my old man? I dunno."

They looked at each other for a few moments. And then Mitch smiled and stood up. He leaned over and grasped Matt's arm in a familiar shake, his hand wrapped around Matt's wrist, Matt's hand around his. "It's been too long," said Mitch.

Matt smiled. "Yeah. Seems like a lifetime ago.

"Get some rest. I'll call in again later." Mitch left the room, closing the door gently behind him.

Matt tried to stay awake to think things through but exhaustion took over and his eyes closed.

Shannon was in the kitchen cradling a cup of tea. Mitch poured himself a coffee from the pot and sat down opposite her at the kitchen table. The tick-tock of the kitchen clock seemed loud in the silence between them.

"He's awake," Mitch told her.

"And?" Shannon studied her cup.

"And I think he's as much of a puppet as I am,"

Shannon frowned at him. "You're not a puppet, Mitch." she said without much expression.

Mitch sipped his coffee. "Lewis Carter wants you for something, Shan. He sent his son to get you on the run. My bet is that he'll swoop in and do his knight-in-white-armor-rescues-damsel-in-distress thing. Get you on his side again before asking for a 'favour'. It's the same old story with a different script."

"I'm no damsel in distress, Mitch. If anyone should know that it's Lewis Carter." Shannon looked away from him again and out of the window. She rested her chin on her hand, lost in a memory, a daydream, whatever it was it shut Mitch out. He studied her profile – the high cheekbones, long aquiline nose, delicate chin and perfect rose-bud lips. She had showered this morning and her jet hair was still damp. It hung down her back, curling gently at the slowly drying ends. Her robe was an old one of his, left behind here several months ago, it was belted as tight as it would go but still hung loose over her slim waist. Mitch frowned, she'd lost more weight. He opened his mouth to say something about it but she turned to him and spoke before he could;

"How's the patient anyway?"

Mitch shrugged. "Seems better, I suppose. Your Doctor pal did a good job. Seems to me he was lucky. I doubt if he'll thank us for it, though."

"Why not? What's his story anyway?" Shannon.

Mitch sighed and refilled both their mugs. "His wife and daughter were killed in a car crash about ten years ago. Well, officially it was a crash. Unofficially it was a clever bomb. It's possible that Matt was the intended target. He'd been running special ops in Iraq for a number of years and he was good, better than good to be honest. He survived the…crash. Emma and Charlene didn't. He basically fell apart, spent four years walking around like a zombie." Mitch stopped and studied his mug.

"Go on," Shannon said softly.

"He was kept on active duty. Maybe because of who his dad was, because he requested it, because they thought it'd be good for him. I dunno. Whatever. The point is that he kept going y'know? He did what he'd been doing but he was detached from it all. He was like a machine – they pointed him at a target, he took it out without any reaction. And then one day he was just gone. Never came back to work. He quit his apartment, quit everything. I heard about him from time to time, you know how it is – a name comes up in conversation – but none of it was good. He ran away from his life and straight into the arms of booze and drugs."

"Cocaine?" Shannon looked shocked.

Mitch laughed. "No. A little pill we found in the desert. It's being trafficked under the name 'Dilysium'. Nasty little thing. Apparently it's hard to refine – get it from the wrong source and you get a ticket straight to hell." He shook his head. "Every one of those you take is like playing Russian Roulette."

He studied Shannon again. She was listening to him but staring past him towards the door. Mitch sighed. "He can handle visitors y'know."

Shannon looked at him guiltily and smiled. "Maybe later. I better get dressed." She rose from the table and headed back to her room.

Mitch sat at the table alone nursing his coffee for a long time.

Chapter Five

Shannon stood in the dimly lit room. She had dressed in jeans and a simple black t-shirt. Her hair was still damp and pulled into a pony tail that hung down to her waist, she toyed with it idly. For the first time since they'd brought him here, Matt Carter's breathing was regular and strong, not the rasped, hitching, shallow breaths she'd become used to. She wondered if he knew that she was here, if he knew that she'd stood here several times before. She wondered if Mitch knew. The thought made her stop playing with her hair for a second and she swallowed audibly. She closed her eyes and drew a shaky breath. She was playing a dangerous game and she wondered, not for the first time, if she was really up to it.

"Shannon?" Matt's voice made her eyes snap open. He was pulling himself up onto the pillows, his eyes tight with the effort.

"Um, yeah, hi." Shannon was looking around the room, trying to find an excuse for being there. She looked, Matt thought, like the proverbial 'rabbit in the headlights'. She moved towards the door. "I'll tell Mitch that you're awake."

"No, wait. I've already spoken to Mitch." Matt reached out a hand and gestured towards the end of the bed. "Sit for a moment." He grinned at her expression. "Really, I could do with the company now that I've counted every faded flower on the wallpaper."

Shannon chewed on her lip for a moment and then sat daintily on the very edge of the corner of the mattress. She kept her head lowered, her eyes on the floor. "How are you feeling?"

"Better. More alive than the last time I spoke to you," Matt answered studying her intently. He had vague memories of her from the house in Portstewart; dark hair, wide mouth, generous lips, small nose and huge grey eyes. She smelled of damp hair from a recent shower and some kind of citrus soap or shampoo. She picked idly at the duvet cover, her eyes straying around the room nervously.

Matt decided to be direct. "I remember you," he said softly.

She looked at him then, her head to the side. Her eyes sharpened and her lips narrowed. "How?"

"You were in an ice cream parlour in a small town called Thompson Falls in Nevada. I think you were around eight years old. You looked small and sad and pretty, sat there amongst all these big men sweating into their suits and talking over and around but never to you."

She blinked. "How do you know this?"

"I was in the car outside. I was eighteen and on my way back to training camp when Dad got the call. I wasn't supposed to be there but you were important and there was no time to leave me anywhere so I had to come. They'd bought you an ice-cream, a big one in a tall frosted glass, but you weren't eating it. You were just sitting on your hands, staring into space and rocking to and fro. Not one of them paid any attention to you."

Shannon licked her bottom lip and sat back a little. "Why should they talk to me? I was just another assignment, another commodity to be transported across the country. At least, that's how it felt for the whole time I was with them."

"How long was that?"

'Ten years. I was eighteen when Mitch brought me to Northern Ireland.'

"And by then the damage was done, right?" Matt grinned at her.

"That's right," Shannon smiled back.

"It can't have been easy. Being raised by…them,"

Shannon shrugged. "They did their best. Three square meals every day, a room of my own, clothes when I needed them, days off."

"But you had handlers?" His voice was gentle but his eyes were probing.

She nodded. "Twenty-four hours a day, seven days a week. They were ok, too, when you got to know them. Anna was in charge from Monday to Thursday with George backing her up. Then Dianne took over from Friday to Sunday. She had Bruno and Davis backing her up." She smiled to herself. "For some reason they seemed to think that I'd be in more danger, or perhaps more dangerous, at weekends."

Matt grinned and struggled to a sitting position. Shannon moved to arrange the pillows behind him. She noticed that there were scars on his back and on his left shoulder. Old scars, fading to thin silver lines. She wrinkled her nose.

"You need a bath," she said, stepping back and sitting down again.

Matt exploded with laughter, holding his stomach. Shannon opened her mouth to apologise but he lifted a hand to stop her.

"Don't apologise. It's refreshing to be faced with the truth for a change and I'm the first to admit that I haven't exactly looked after myself much just lately. I know I had a shower one morning but I'm not sure which morning. To be honest I can't remember if that was in my apartment, a hotel or …" he stopped. "Sorry. I'm rambling. It's been a while since my head was this clear."

"How does it feel?"

"Not as bad as I expected." Matt shifted on the bed again.

Shannon frowned. "Are you ok?"

"Um, yeah, well. I just need to…y'know?"

Shannon looked at him for a second, bewildered and then understanding flowed into her eyes. "OH!" she exclaimed. "Well, it's just along the hall. I can help you there," she stood up and moved towards him.

"Er, thanks but maybe I should try it myself," said Matt.

"What? Don't be ridiculous. You've been really ill. I'll help." Shannon lifted the edge of the duvet and was about to pull it off him when he pushed her hand away with more force than he'd imagined himself capable. Shannon raised an eyebrow.

"I'm not really, well, I'm kind of…" Matt stuttered.

"What?" said Shannon, exasperated, "What is it? Spit it out!"

Matt managed to swing his knees under him and sat up on the bed, his face inches from her. He was embarrassed and annoyed. "I'm naked!" he growled at her.

Shannon blinked once, twice, three times. "Oh, ok." she backed away. "I'll get Mitch to get you some clothes and show you where the bathroom is."

"Thank you!" said Matt, sinking back onto the bed in relief as she closed the door softly behind her.

Chapter Six

On the fifth day of their stay in the farmhouse, Matt made it downstairs on shaky legs. The place was old and full of creaking floorboards, peeling wallpaper and odd twists and turns. The low ceilings gave him a problem too. Every time he ducked to avoid banging his head, his vision swam and made him feel nauseous. Most of the rooms he looked into as he passed were bare. They smelled of dust and abandonment. It seemed that only a few rooms facing away from the small dirt road and the drive were furnished and even then only sparsely.

He paused in the living room. Dusk was falling, casting shadows around the walls and filling him with a familiar sense of dread and loneliness. He took several deep breaths and followed the only source of light and conversation into the kitchen.

The kitchen was large and typical for an old farmhouse – full of furniture that was useful but wouldn't win any design prizes. There was a stove, acres of worktop space a couple of badly upholstered chairs and a large rectangular table. A radio was playing softly and Mitch was sitting at the far end of the table reading a book. He stood up when Matt opened the door, an initial look of alarm turning to delight.

"Hey! The invalid finally made it downstairs. Have a seat big man." He pulled a chair from under the table and Matt eased himself into it gratefully. He'd broken into a sweat just by walking downstairs.

"I must be really outta shape – can't even walk down a few stairs now," he said.

Mitch grinned at him and went to fill the kettle at the heavy Belfast sink. "Coffee? It's usually a wee cup of tea in this part of the world but Shannon still stuck to her coffee. It's becoming such a habit now that I usually unpack the coffee jar before the tea bags. My auld Ma would be turning in her grave if she saw that." They laughed and the old house's pipes wheezed and spluttered before disgorging enough water to fill the kettle. There was a comfortable silence until two cups of coffee were sitting in front of them.

"Do you miss Dublin?" asked Matt.

Mitch considered it for a moment. 'No," he said finally, "I left a long time ago. When Mam died and the house was sold, well, I didn't really have much of a reason to go back."

"And Sean?" asked Matt. "He was asking about you." He sipped his coffee, concentrating on keeping his hand steady as he lifted the mug.

Mitch glanced in his direction and then sighed. He pushed his book away and studied his hands. "I've never been any good, Matt. Sean knows I'll never be the Dad that he wants. Grace married again so he has a step-dad and all that stuff. I phone him every year on his birthday but only because I know he'll be sitting waiting. I thought he'd grow out of it but…" He stood up and busied himself with filling the kettle again. "How was he anyway?" he asked.

"He's good. He's grown into a fine man, Mitch. Looks like you too."

Mitch nodded, a slow smile spreading across his face. "God help the young women of Dublin as another Connor makes his way through them, eh?"

Matt nodded slowly. "He's working for the dissidents," he said, his eyes watching Mitch carefully.

His words had the effect he'd expected. Mitch's smile faded. "Where?"

"All over. They're careful and they're clever."

Mitch pursed his lips. "How did you find out? You couldn't have been there more than a few hours and the state you were in…"

"Blade was in his house. There was talk"

Silence filled the room.

Mitch reached for Matt's cup, refilled it and pushed it back across the table. "I didn't know that butcher was still alive. No doubt he was round handing out orders."

Matt shrugged. "As you say, I wasn't there for long, and I wasn't exactly able to pay much attention but…" he paused.

"Just tell me," Mitch leaned across the table a little, his eyes sparkling dangerously.

Matt sighed. "Well, it seemed to me that Blade was taking orders from Sean."

Mitch rose from the table, his mouth open to retort, when the back door opened and Shannon rocketed in, panting hard. Her hair was scraped back in a severe pony tail and she was wearing tight black cycling shorts and a long baggy sweatshirt. Her iPod was still switched on and so loud that Matt had no problem making out the words to Def Leppard's 'Animal'.

Shannon stopped and studied the scene. Her mouth formed a small 'o' of understanding and she switched off the music. "I can do another few miles, give you guys some more time to talk," she said softly, looking from one to the other.

Mitch waved the idea away. "No, come on in. We've discussed all that needed to be discussed anyway." He gestured towards the coffee pot. "Coffee's fresh."

Shannon glanced briefly at Matt – checking his feelings on the matter, he thought – and then she nodded, walked over to the wall and began a series of cooling down stretches. All in all it took about ten minutes, during which Matt watched Shannon and Mitch watched Matt, a thoughtful smile on his face.

At the end of her stretches, Shannon sat down on the floor, facing Matt. She put the soles of her feet together and her elbows on the inside of her knees. Leaning forward she gradually pressed her knees towards the ground.

Matt knew that his mouth was hanging open but he couldn't seem to get his mind away from the sight of her long, lean legs in the skimpy shorts. Sensing his scrutiny, Shannon looked up at him. "You're up." she said.

"Huh?!" was all Matt could manage. On the other side of the table, Mitch sniggered into his coffee. "Er, yeah. I guess I am," Matt said.

There was an embarrassed silence and then, after a confused glance in Matt's direction, Shannon mercifully stood up and left the room. Matt ran a hand through his hair and blew out his cheeks. He looked at Mitch who was grinning at him. "Don't say it," said Matt.

"Say what?"

"I acted like a sixteen year old."

Mitch laughed. "She has that affect, Matt. Don't worry about it." He picked up his book and began to read. Matt stretched out in the chair, his long legs crossed at his ankles. Before long the heat of the kitchen had him almost drifting into a doze. The kitchen door opened again and Shannon came back into the room. She had changed into a night-shirt and a large, fluffy blue robe that might once have been Mitch's. Her hair was damp, loose and tumbling over her shoulders. She accepted a coffee from Mitch with a smile and sat down without glancing in Matt's direction.

Mitch looked from Matt to Shannon and began to fill the uncomfortable silence – he talked about his childhood in Dublin, the beatings from his father, the intense love he felt for his mother, the last photograph he remembered her taking of himself and his brothers on the fire escape of their building a few minutes' walk from O'Connell Station.

"I was fourteen, the youngest, and I felt like the luckiest git in the whole city. There I was with the two best lookin' lads in Dublin and they were my brothers. I was proud, so bloody proud. It's the last time we were all together, the last time I heard them laugh, whispering dirty jokes to me as Mam sorted the camera out. We were crazy, expecting to spend the rest of our lives chasing girls and getting into fights with the arseholes from the other side of the bridge. Little did we know, eh?" He smiled wistfully. "Christ, I sound like an auld boy of ninety!" They all laughed. "What about you, Matt? Any poignant thoughts on growing up?" Mitch sat back in his chair and reached into his pocket for a packet of cigarettes. He offered them round the table but Shannon and Matt both refused.

Matt tensed. Talking about his childhood meant travelling back over memories that were better left untouched. He coughed into his hand. "What's to tell that you don't already know? My dad was a big shot in the Bureau and now he's a big shot in the Senate. He wanted the same for me – set me on the right road form the age of about six, introduced me to the right people, enrolled me in the right schools, dressed me in the right suits." He paused and his mouth twitched. "Didn't help did it?"

"You were in the Panthers with Mitch, weren't you?" asked Shannon. Matt nodded mutely. "Well, surely you couldn't have gotten that far without ability?"

"You don't know the half of it, Shan," said Mitch, leaning his elbows on the table and looking at Matt through a haze of smoke. "This guy…" he pointed towards him with his cigarette,"…he was tough and sharp." He tapped his temple. "He had it all up here, brains to burn."

"Yeah," said Matt, his voice hard edged, "And I reckon I've just about burned them all away by now. Along with everyone I cared about."

Mitch looked at him carefully over the rim of his cup. He dropped his gaze when Matt turned in his direction. There was very little to say to that.

Shannon blew out a long breath and dropped her head back. "Bored already," she mumbled.

Both men turned to look at her. Matt's face twisted in surprise, Mitch's eyes wide.

"What did you say?" Matt's voice was low, almost a growl.

Shannon sighed and stood up, pouring herself another coffee. "Look, I'm sure you've had a tough time; lost people you care about, feel like a failure in your Dad's eyes, yadda, yadda, yadda. How long ago was this tragedy?" She looked at Mitch.

"Eight years," Mitch said, glancing from Shannon to Matt.

"Yeah, so eight years is a long time to be feeling sorry for yourself. I mean, you're a big, black ops tough guy; you're trained to cope with pretty much everything. Plus your Dad's a big wheel in, well, in every place that matters so you have contacts comin' out of your ears. I just don't see what your problem is." She sat down.

Matt was incredulous. His head was pounding and he dug his fingernails into the palms of his hands to keep from reaching across and throttling her. "The problem?" his voice was barely a whisper. "The problem is that the person I strove to become to make my father happy is the very reason why I lost the only two things that really mattered. I killed my wife and daughter as surely as I put my gun to their heads and pulled the trigger." He shook his head, the anger dying away as anguish took over. "I killed my family."

If all his attention hadn't been focused on her in that split second, he might have missed it. As it was he caught her glance in Mitch's direction. It was the kind of rapid side-of-the-eye peek that a child gives its parents in the midst of a temper tantrum. An 'are-they-watching-this-performance?' kind of look; as though she was trying to persuade Mitch that she didn't like Matt. What the hell?

And then Shannon was speaking, her attention back on him. "I killed mine too," she said.

Chapter Seven

"That's a story for another day, I think." She busied herself rinsing her mug, setting it on the draining board, searching in the drawer for a tea-towel to dry it.

Matt looked hard at Mitch but his face remained expressionless. Finally Matt pulled himself out of the chair and walked over to the sink. This close she smelled of citrus again and coffee. "I'd like to know." He said softly.

Shannon turned to him, her eyes bore into his. "I don't trust you," she said and turned back to the sink.

Matt sighed. He looked out into the darkness beyond the window and began to recite, "Special Agent Anna Davis, died in an R.T.A. Special Agent George Maxwell died in a house fire, Special Agent Dianne Harris OD'd on a drug that no-one prescribed for her, Special Agent Bruno Miller died R.T.A., Special Agent David Simpson died in a drive-by. Wrong place, wrong time apparently."

Shannon had turned slowly to face him, tears in her eyes. She shook her head, looked towards Mitch and then back at Matt. "Andy?" she asked in a breathless, horrified voice.

"Special Agent Andrew Graham, died in a burglary at his residence almost three weeks ago."

Shannon sat down heavily, the tea-towel still in her hands. A tear spilled out of her right eye and slid slowly down her cheek. She swallowed. "How do you know this?" she asked levelly.

"My dad." Matt said. "You know, the one with all the contacts in the right places?" His voice dripped sarcasm. "When he came to drag me out of my apartment and send me after you, he stayed just long enough to pass on some pertinent information. Now, I don't know what you do, I don't know why you were still in contact with these people if you no longer work for the Bureau." He looked at her carefully but her expression was blank. "I don't know who killed them or why but I do know that my dad didn't believe that their deaths were a coincidence. What do you think?"

Shannon looked up at him. Her expression was carefully neutral but her eyes were shadowy pools of pain and anger. She opened her mouth to speak but darted a glance in Mitch's direction again and said nothing. She looked back at Matt, deep into his eyes for a moment and he got the message. Not in front of Mitch.

And then Mitch spoke. "I can vouch for him, Shan. Why don't you tell him?"

Shannon looked at Mitch and then at her hands, jumbled up in the tea towel. "Fine, she said. "But I'm going to need something stronger than coffee."

They moved from the kitchen to the mismatched but comfortable chairs of the living room. Mitch poured them all a generous measure of Bushmills whiskey and then sat down, his eyes moving from Matt to Shannon.

Shannon bit her lip. "I don't know where to start," she admitted, her voice a whisper. She took a gulp of the whiskey, shivered as the taste hit the back of her throat and then sighed as the warmth spread through her body. She looked over at Matt and took a deep breath. "How much do you know about 'Project Stargate'?"

Matt frowned. "I take it we aren't talking about the TV series?" Shannon raised an eyebrow and he grinned. "Sorry, couldn't resist." He paused and thought for a moment. "Project Stargate was some kind of umbrella code-name for a lot of projects that the government ran. Something to do with psychic phenomena. They were all closed down by the mid-nineties I think." He looked up at her again. "How'd I do?"

Shannon smiled. "Most of the details of Stargate were declassified after it was transferred to the CIA in 1995. The project was closed on 30th June that year just before evaluations by the American Institutes for Research was due to begin. At its peak, the government was throwing 20million dollars per year at it and there were maybe 14 labs researching just one of the sub-projects. The lab that I was connected to was called "Silver Sands" and the project the Sands lab worked on was remote viewing." She looked at Matt under her lashes. He looked to be deep in thought, his brow furrowed as he stared off into space somewhere just past her shoulder. At her sudden silence he glanced back at her. "You're not freaking out yet?"

Matt shook his head. "Not yet. I take it that you were a remote viewer then? Go on."

"The Silver Sands lab wasn't on any documentation that was ever released within the hallowed halls of the CIA or to any of the main project personnel."

"Why? What was the big deal if there was so much money being pumped into it?" Matt asked.

"Well, I think it was because, in the other projects the remote viewers were right maybe 20% of the time."

"And you?"

Shannon's smile was caught somewhere between pride and embarrassment. "I had, and still have, a 100% record." She opened her mouth to talk again but Matt interrupted.

"Wait. You said you 'still' have a 100% record? I thought the project was closed down."

Shannon nodded. "Well, officially Project Stargate shut down, yes. Silver Sands lab was given over to other projects and all the others still within the sub-projects moved on, went back to their civilian lives, or were re-assigned." She shifted uneasily in the chair. "I was never officially a part of anything so I was never decommissioned. I was, however, given a new identity and a… guardian angel," she smiled at Mitch. "But I am still an active."

Matt shook his head. "I don't buy this. No active like you stays secret and hidden for almost ten years."

"I'm only called when all the other avenues have been explored. I'm the last resort. And I'm not clairvoyant so I can't see where someone or something is going to be, I can only see where they are at this moment in time. Sometimes that's not very useful." Shannon sighed.

"But all the people who know about you?" Matt argued, "The people you work with, the people they answer to. How do you stay out of that loop?"

"Andy Graham was my contact. We met once in the last ten years. Everything else has been done by encoded message. Anna, George, Dianne, Bruno and David," Shannon sighed, "As my ex-guards they were sworn to secrecy under the terms of national security. You know how that is. They were only to provide possible safe houses if necessary..." her voice trailed off and she bit her lip, frowning, as though something had just occurred to her.

"Shan?" Mitch asked gently.

With an effort she snapped back to them. "Yes, sorry. Just hard to imagine they're all gone." She grimaced.

"So, who did you meet with? When you had a job on, I mean?" Matt pushed again.

"I don't know. We always wore masks, sent to us by Andy I think. He had a weird sense of humour. Once we were all ex-presidents. Once we were all Marilyn Monroe. Last time it was a freaky Halloween theme." She shook her head, smiling. "You haven't lived till you've seen a room full of men in swat gear wearing Marilyn faces complete with platinum blonde hair." Her face grew serious again. "You don't think there was a way to track them down, tie them to me somehow?"

Matt frowned. "You think someone is taking out your team?"

"Don't you?" Shannon's eyes were clear and focused, boring into him.

Matt held her gaze for a moment and then shrugged. "Dunno. Who gains from that?"

Mitch stood up, yawning and stretching. "Someone with a bitch against Stargate? Tying up loose ends? Who knows? C'mon guys, let's hit the hay. Maybe we'll be able to figure this out in the morning after the alcoholic haze has lifted and we've had some sleep."

Matt looked at his glass and was surprised to find it empty. He had no memory of drinking it but his head felt happily fuzzy. He grinned to himself. There would be no problem falling asleep tonight. He pulled himself to his feet and stretched, feeling his aching muscles stretch and twinge.

Mitch was leading Shannon from the room, an arm slung casually over her shoulders. "G'night, Matt," he said from the door, yawning around the words.

Matt grinned. "'Night, Mitch."

Shannon turned under Mitch's arm to look back at him. "Do

you have any way to get in touch with your dad?" she asked and Matt could've sworn he saw Mitch flinch.

He shook his head. "Not really. I thought I'd brought my cell but I must've dropped it somewhere or left it in the car in Portstewart." He made a face. "Guess I really was out of it."

Shannon nodded and smiled but her eyes were troubled and dark as she slid back into Mitch's embrace.

Matt followed them upstairs and waved from the door of his room, pausing as he turned the handle to see whether or not they went into the same room. He was curious at the sudden show of affection. At his door, Mitch whispered something into Shannon's ear, a playful smile on his lips. Shannon returned his smile but kissed him gently on the cheek and slipped from under his arm and through the opposite door. Mitch stood for a moment watching her door close and then opened his own door, giving Matt a wry shrug before he went inside and closed it with a dull thud.

Almost immediately Shannon's door opened again and she peeked out. Matt looked up at her in surprise. She held a finger to her lips and pointed at Mitch's door. Matt nodded his understanding. She pointed at him and then made a phone shape with her right hand - her thumb at her ear and her little finger at her mouth - pointed to the pocket of her jeans and then back at Mitch's room.

Matt frowned in thought, studying his feet. The penny dropped and he looked up at her. Her face was clouded with uncertainty and perhaps a touch of fear. She glanced at Mitch's door and, with a final look in Matt's direction, retreated into her room and quietly shut the door.

Matt sat down on the edge of his bed and tried to make his brain work. His head felt as though it was cocooned in cotton wool and his eyes were hot and heavy. He flopped back onto the bed, his legs hanging off the bottom. As sleep took over his brain registered three things. One, according to Shannon, he had had a cell phone with him, two, she believed that Mitch had taken it and three, she was afraid of Mitch.

Chapter Eight

For the next few days Mitch was jolly and attentive, happy to reminisce about their shared past, places they had been, operations they had taken part in. Together he and Matt downed the rest of the whiskey and Matt felt his body and mind heal a little more. Shannon was a ghost - her presence in the house barely registering as she flitted from room to room, from jogging sessions to trips out for supplies. When she was around her reaction to Matt was frosty and reserved, keeping a distance between them. With Mitch she was calm, relaxed and content. His arm appeared around her shoulder more often or slipped around her waist as she washed dishes at the sink. Each time, she looked up at him with an expression bordering on adoration, her eyes sparkling and a smile playing about her lips.

Matt was beginning to feel like an unwanted chaperone, until their last evening in the farmhouse, when he found her in the kitchen scrubbing her hands until they were red raw and sobbing quietly.

Mitch had gone to put diesel in the car. They had packed during the day, putting everything they needed into three battered old cases. Matt was surprised to find that Shannon had shopped for him, buying new clothes, soap, toothpaste and brush, shaving essentials and even a cheap, but functional, watch . He had brought his case downstairs, put it beside the other two and then realized that Mitch had gone. Seizing the opportunity, he had gone looking for Shannon – there were things they needed to discuss without Mitch around.

She jumped guiltily when he came into the kitchen and then turned away from him, wiping her tears on the sleeve of her light blue shirt. Matt frowned. "Did he hurt you?" he growled.

Shannon laughed hoarsely. "No, of course not."

"So what happened?" Matt turned her to face him and lifted her hands up to examine them. Apart from the fierce scrubbing that she had given them, they appeared to be unharmed. He turned them over, looking for cuts or scars. There was nothing.

He looked up at her questioningly.

Shannon took a shuddering breath and pulled her hands from his, drying them on a tea towel and wiping her eyes again. "Nothing happened," she said tonelessly.

"Shannon," Matt warned. "I can't help you, if you don't tell me what's going on," He turned her to face him again, his hands on her shoulders as he studied her face.

Shannon closed her eyes. "Devil's and dust," she whispered.

Matt screwed up his face. "Sorry, you've lost me."

"It's like the Springsteen song, Devils and Dust. There's this line in it – "I've got my finger on the trigger…"she began.

"..But I don't know who to trust…" Matt finished.

She grinned at him. "Yeah."

Matt sighed. "What happened?" he asked again.

Shannon bit her lip. Matt's hands were warm on her shoulders, his brown eyes looked sincere and she very much needed him to be on her side. He hadn't said anything to Mitch about his cell and she'd given him plenty of opportunity, so maybe she should take the chance and confide in him. On the other hand, he could be in on this with Mitch and they could be playing her to see how much she knew. She could find herself well and truly screwed.

Matt could see the conflict washing across her face so he waited.

"He kissed the back of my hands," Shannon said matter-of-factly. "Before he left in the car, he kissed my hands. So I had to wash them."

Matt opened his mouth, closed it again. "That was SO not what I was expecting," He said finally. He frowned. "I thought you two were, well, pretty close."

Shannon smiled grimly, "It's not all how it looks, Matt," she said.

With that the back door opened and Mitch came in, whistling. He stopped when he saw Matt and Shannon. Matt followed the line of Mitch's gaze and dropped his hands from Shannon's shoulders. He grinned guiltily at Mitch. "I was just thanking Shannon for helping me get back on my feet and getting me the new clothes and stuff," Matt said.

Mitch dropped a bag of shopping on the kitchen table. He raised an eyebrow at Matt. "You gonna thank me with a hug too?" he asked.

Matt grinned, "Nah. You're not pretty enough," he quipped.

Mitch rolled his eyes. "Let's put the bags in the car. I want to get underway. We're expected in Dublin by tomorrow." He looked at Shannon. "And I think Matt's getting way too fresh with my best girl!"

Shannon managed a weak smile as Matt laughed heartily and went to pick up the cases in the hall. Mitch waited until he was out of ear hot and then smiled at her. "Sorry you had to put up with that, Shan. Next time he gets all clingy I'll shoot him." He laughed and went to help Matt, leaving Shannon biting on her lip in the kitchen.

Chapter Nine

Matt was loading the last case into the car at the rear of the farmhouse when he heard the engine. He slammed the boot and moved to the side of the house. The car, a black Mercedes, was making its way along the bumpy country road. He ducked back into the shadows and listened. It was moving away from them. He risked a look towards the road. The Mercedes had gone past the end of the drive that led up to the house. As he watched the brake lights came on and the car stopped.

For a moment it just sat there. He imagined the occupants debating what to do. It was fairly obvious that they weren't on a main road. Or a road that went anywhere but further up a twisty trail to the top of a hill - sixteen miles, passing through arable land with maybe one more crumbling house and a couple of cow sheds .Ahead, the trail was clear as far as the eye could see and, if the occupants of the car had followed Mitch there, they would be fairly certain that his Corsa hadn't gone any further.

It began to rain, fat droplets hitting the dry ground with soft splats. Matt closed his eyes for a second and turned his face up to the sky. The rain was getting heavier. He pushed his hair out of his eyes and turned his attention back to the car. The occupants had obviously made a decision, the car was reversing. A part of his sub-conscious was telling him that the people driving towards the house could simply be lost, would ask for directions and then be on their way. The rest of him was screaming danger - a sixth sense kicking back into action and pushing him to be ready.

Matt checked his glock. He had found it earlier in the day, wrapped in a new shirt in one of the drawers in his room. It was one of the things he'd wanted to ask Shannon about when he'd found her crying in the kitchen. The weapon was ready for action. Matt's heart was hammering in his chest, adrenaline surging through him in anticipation. Christ, he thought, what a time to start worrying about having a heart attack.

The car slid to a stop at the bottom of the lane and turned slowly up towards the house. Matt knew he should let Mitch and

Shannon know but he was wary of taking his eyes off the car. He scanned the yard for cover in case he had to leave his place at the wall. There was none. It was a small front yard with three planters containing long-dead flowers of some kind and an old bicycle slowly depositing its rust on the concrete.

The car stopped at the top of the drive and then manoeuvred until the nose was pointing back down towards the road again. Whoever was in the car was obviously expecting some kind of trouble if they had taken the time to prepare for a fast getaway. Matt sneaked a look around the front of the house. There was a soft glow through the main door but the front porch was in thick shadow. Matt cursed under his breath and slid back around the corner. He had hoped that either Mitch or Shannon would have come to check what was taking him so long. Out of the corner of his eye, he caught movement from the back of the house and his head snapped up. A figure darted towards the fields that bordered the house and into cover of the thick hedge. Matt raised his gun and then realized that he was aiming at Mitch. He lowered the gun again, cautioning himself to be cool, be calm.

There was a creak and moan and both of the car's back doors opened. Matt hunkered down. He could see Mitch's dark form moving along the hedge until he was behind the car. Two men had emerged from the back seat. Both wore unremarkable clothes – jeans and jackets. They gave the yard a cursory glance and then headed for the house. Matt realized that Shannon was alone in there. Cursing softly he stood up and turned around, finding himself level with a grimy window, propped open by an old brush shaft. Moving more swiftly than he would have imagined himself capable of a few days earlier, he quickly but quietly eased the window up a little further and then pulled himself through.

The house was quiet and the room was dark and full of disturbed dust. Matt smothered a sneeze and moved to the door, easing it open until he could see into the corridor beyond. The hall was dimly lit by a bare bulb, heavy with grime. He was debating whether to move towards the kitchen when the hall vibrated with the thud, thud, thud of a fist on the front door. Matt gritted his teeth and gripped his gun a little tighter.

A door opened at the far end of the hall and Shannon came out, wrapping the old blue robe around her and straightening a platinum blond wig. She pushed his door closed a she passed.

"Stay in there," she hissed.

Matt flattened himself against the wall, his heart hammering in fear for her. His eyes darted back and forth in the gloom, searching for some idea of how to help. The dark, empty room glared back at him. He heard muffled voices and moved closer to the door. The two men were asking about another farm in the area, talking in clipped English accents. Shannon was telling them that the nearest farm was almost five miles to the West, using a strong local accent. Matt grinned. Multi-talented! He was impressed.

The two men were moving slowly down the hall as they chatted. Shannon noticed but pretended not to, clutching nervously at the edges of her robe as though embarrassed to be caught in it. The man on her left was looking surreptitiously towards the room where Matt had hidden himself. She assumed that they intended to overpower her and then search the house. Thanks to Matt sneaking in she would have no second chances, her first moves would have to count. Matt's door opened just a crack, if either of the men glanced in that direction again then he would be seen. Cursing him inwardly she took a deep breath and dropped her robe open.

Standing at the crack in the door, Matt stared for a moment his mouth gaping. She hadn't just done that, had she? And she was wearing…he looked away, the impression of black lace and creamy skin seared onto the back of his eyeballs. He squeezed his eyes shut and shook his head. Shannon had obviously had the same impression on the two men. They stood gawping, eyes wide and jaws dropping to the floor.

Shannon moved while their eyes were still glued to her cleavage. The flat of her hand caught the nearest man across the bridge of his nose, breaking it instantly. His hands moved to cup his face and she struck again, kicking his mid-section and winding him. As he doubled up in agony she delivered a blow to the side of his neck. He crumpled to the floor and lay still.

Matt had recovered from the shock as soon as he saw Shannon's first strike. Training took over and he was through the door in an instant, grabbing the man in front of him around the neck just as he was going for a weapon inside his jacket. They grappled for a moment, twisting this way and that. Matt pulled up sharply and the man began to gasp for breath, his hands pulling ineffectually at the vice-like arm around his throat.

As Shannon's first mark fell to the ground she swung back around and delivered a kick to the groin of the man in Matt's grasp. He sagged, moaning and Shannon struck again, her hand slicing into his windpipe just as Matt let go.

They stood for a moment their breathing loud in the now-silent house. The back door opened and Matt swung his gun towards it, pulling Shannon behind him. Mitch held up his hands and surveyed the hall. "Looks like I missed all the fun," he said with a wide grin. He looked back to Shannon and Matt, his eyes raking over her current state of undress. "Wow, maybe I didn't miss all the fun yet." He lifted an eyebrow and licked his lips.

Matt was suddenly very aware of Shannon pressed against his side, one of her hands wrapped around the top of his arm. He had pushed her with his left hand which was still on her thigh, tickled by a stay inch of lace. He glanced at her but her focus was on Mitch, her face flaming. Matt slowly moved his hand away and turned back to the mocking smile on Mitch's face.

"Were there others?" he asked.

Mitch nodded. "Two in the car." He mimed pulling a trigger at his head.

"You killed them?" Matt was aghast.

Mitch frowned at him. "They were armed and after us. What did you want me to do? Invite them in for tea and cake?"

"How do you know they were after us?" asked Matt, his anger rising. "We don't kill innocent people, Mitch."

"Oh, really? Don't give me the whole holier-than-thou speech, Carter. You've taken lives, just like I have."

"Only when the threat was proven."

Mitch narrowed his eyes and took a step forward. "Proven by what? An order from someone on the other side of the world?" He shook his head and made a disgusted noise. "That's always been your problem, Matt."

Matt moved forward too, stepping over the man at his feet. "What problem would that be?"

They were within reach of each other, eyes blazing. Shannon's grip tightened on Matt's arm and he looked down, surprised that she was still holding onto him. "Much as I'm enjoying this little display of testosterone, please could we deal with the matter at hand?" She gestured around the hall.

"There's a disused quarry to the east, we can dump them and the car there. They probably called this in. I reckon we have about thirty minutes." Mitch said, reaching for the body closest to him.

"These men aren't dead, Mitch. We're not dumping them in a quarry." Matt said, his voice hard and flat.

Mitch sighed. "OK, Snow White. We'll leave them there in their car so they can live to hunt us down and kill us another day. Ok? You've changed, man." He slung the prone body onto his back and pushed past them to the door.

Matt cursed and reached behind himself to tuck his gun into the waistband of his jeans. Then he knelt down and gently lifted the second man into his arms and carried him into the car. Mitch had already moved the driver into the back and was slipping behind the wheel. "Pick me up at the quarry, Shannon should have a rough idea where it is." he said. Matt was trying not to notice the blood splattered on the passenger window.

"Mitch..." Matt began.

Mitch waved away whatever he had been going to say. "Yeah, yeah, don't kill them, I know, I know. What's the matter, Matt? Don't you trust me?" He drove away at speed, spraying stones as he slid onto the road.

Shannon and Matt locked up the house quickly and drove away from the farmhouse. "Nice moves back there," Matt told her to break the silence.

She looked at him.

"I mean the...y'know..." he mimed a karate chop and she nodded, grinning.

"I thought you meant the..." she mimed dropping her robe.

Matt grinned. "Well, that was nice too," he admitted and tried to concentrate on the road. He grew serious again. "We could just keep driving y'know."

Shannon chewed on her lip. "Yes, we could." she said softly.

"There's a silent 'but' tagged on there," Matt carefully kept his eyes on the road.

Shannon shifted in her seat, sneaking a glance at him. "Yeah, and several 'what-if's' with a few billion 'maybes.'" She wrapped her arms around herself and sank further into her seat. "And then there are also a few really unexpected twists and turns. Like you."

Matt looked at her then, caught her eyes and held them for a split second. "Next left." She told him.

Matt made the turn and they travelled the rest of the way in silence, both lost in a fog of unspoken questions and confusion. Mitch was waiting for them at the quarry, leaning on the Mercedes with a practiced air of nonchalance. Matt pulled up a few feet away and killed the engine.

"I want to know what I'm in the middle of," he whispered urgently to Shannon as he clambered into the back seat. She nodded, a brief inclination of her head and then greeted Mitch with a bright smile.

"Still wearing your glad rags under those jeans, princess?" asked Mitch as they left the quarry, he glanced in the rear-view at Matt's reaction and chuckled as Matt refused to meet his eyes.

Shannon smiled tightly. "You're in a good mood." she remarked.

"Yeah, a good fight always did that for me."

"No," said Shannon carefully, "You were stoked even before that."

Mitch's smile widened. "I always said you were a bright spark, princess. Yeah, I'm having a good day. Took a call from Sean this morning. He's managed to get us a flight out from Shannon in about eight days. We'll be staying down there with them until it's all settled."

Shannon sat up a little straighter in her chair, she licked her lips anxiously. "Really?" She was glad her voice was steady. "Is Dublin safe for you?"

Mitch made a face. "Well, it is and it isn't. We're in luck 'though. Sean's got the city by the short and curlies so he'll look out for us, keep us away from the ould boys."

Shannon was frowning and Matt could feel her fear from where he was sitting. She made a visible effort to pull herself together. "And if I don't want to go?"

Mitch turned to her in astonishment. "Why wouldn't you? Dunlin's a fine city. Plenty of shopping which I seem to remember you enjoying once upon a time. Sean's living with his girl, Erin, so you'll have some female company for a change too. It's all good, Shan." He reached out and brushed his knuckles across her cheekbone, an unconsciously aggressive gesture that made Matt's hands curl into fists.

Shannon looked out of her window for a while. "Sean doesn't like me."

Mitch made a tutting noise. "For God's sake. You only met him once and it was a good while ago. He's grown up, Shan. Give him a chance. Besides, it's not forever is it?"

She turned to face him again. "So, it's just for eight days and then we fly out?" Mitch nodded, grinning. "Where are we flying to?"

Mitch laughed. "Ah, now that would be telling. It's a surprise."

"I thought Dublin was safe," Matt said from the back seat. "Why not just stay there?" Shannon shot him a dark look.

"Hmmm, well, I'm kind of well-known in my hometown, Matt. If there are people looking for us out there, then that's probably going to be the first place they'll look. Sean'll have some tricks up his sleeve but they won't last for long and we can't really ask him to put the three of us up forever, can we?. Best to get out as soon as possible." He reached over and squeezed Shannon's hand. "You'd like a trip, wouldn't you, honey?"

Shannon smiled crookedly at him. "I'd like to know where I'm going – I mean, if we're going to be skiing I'd like to be prepared."

Mitch laughed again. "Maybe I'll tell you nearer the time," he lifted her hand to his lips and planted a kiss in the centre of her palm. "In the meantime, why don't you get some rest?"

Shannon leaned back in her seat and turned her head towards the window. To Mitch it might have looked as though she was sleeping but Matt could see her face in the side mirror – her lips were pressed angrily together and her eyes were blazing. Matt puzzled over it all – Shannon's story of being an active agent was warped on many levels, but she had handled the two men in the farmhouse so for now he was willing to believe that she was telling the truth. So where did Mitch fit in? And Lewis Carter, his father? She and Mitch had obviously once been…close - Mitch obviously still believed that they were. So why was she so angry with him, so worried about being in Dublin? Matt frowned as his brain sorted through all the possibilities and, as the car reached a main road and began to eat up the miles, he fell asleep.

Chapter Ten

Matt was aware of someone shaking him. He gasped and tried to stand, banging his head on the ceiling of the car and knocking his shoulder on the seat in front.

"Ow!" He complained.

"Wakey, wakey, Sleeping Beauty. We have new wheels." Mitch was leaning into the back of the Corsa. He pointed to a dark blue Mondeo parked in front of them and they all piled into it.

Matt offered to drive and, after a brief hesitation, Mitch agreed. He settled down in the back seat and was snoring within minutes.

"Hope you know the way to Dublin," Matt stage-whispered.

Shannon shrugged. "I think I can keep us in the right general direction." She directed him back onto the M1 motorway and they were soon heading south again.

"So, tell me something about you that I don't know," Matt said, with a glance in Mitch's direction.

Shannon laughed dryly. "Which of the three billion things that you don't know about me would you like to start with?"

"Hmmm. Well, you know all about me and my family. Why don't you tell me about yours? Your childhood. That kind of thing."

Shannon frowned and took a deep breath. She studied her hands for a moment and finally she said. "My name wasn't always Shannon Reeves. I was given a new identity when Stargate closed. Before that my name was Rebecca Morgan." She waited. Matt reacted in exactly the way she imagined he would. He turned to face her, his eyes wide. His mouth opened and closed several times. Shannon pointed to the road. "We drive on the left, here." she told him.

Matt pulled the car back into the left lane. "You're the 'Orphan Heiress'?" he asked in astonishment. Shannon winced. "Sorry," he looked away from her, looked back and then looked away again.

Shannon folded her hands in her lap and studied her nails for a moment. "My dad worked for the government on the weapons program. He was away a lot and my mum, well, she was really into being rich so she was always at lunches and benefits and spa days. I had an older sister called Sophie and an older brother called David." He voice cracked slightly on her brother's name and Matt glanced at her sharply but she went on. "We were always close, thick as thieves. I suppose we gave each other the hugs and kisses and a million other little things that our parents weren't there for. I walked earlier than my siblings, spoke much earlier too and my ability to process information, to retain it and use it to make sense of the world was way beyond my years. My dad decided that I was a gifted child. I was his party piece." She smiled at the memory.

Her face darkened. "And then I began to talk about things that I couldn't possibly know about, things I couldn't simply have picked up. He lost a file for a company that he was investigating. When he came to my room to kiss me goodnight I was able to tell him which drawer of his filing cabinet it was in. I was only three years old and I'd never been to his office. I told him that one of his colleagues had been caught in an RTA within minutes of it happening. There were other things but they're not important. The point is that my dad took me for tests. My abilities spooked him but also intrigued him so the tests were done by a friend of his, a psychologist called Isaac Rosen. Rosen was a calm, quiet man who treated me very kindly. But he also passed on my information to a scientist who was part of the Stargate project. Within a year I was being studied by this second scientist in tandem with Dr Rosen."

"Did they hurt you?" Matt interrupted, his voice gentle but angry.

Shannon shook her head. "No, not really. I was bored more than anything. It was always the same. They gave me a photograph or a brush, bracelet, old shirt...whatever. And I would tell them what I could see, sense, feel. Most of the time they would just smile, pat me on the back and give me a treat. Sometimes they couldn't hide their exhilaration. I thought they were weird, high-fiving each other and buying me dolls." She grinned. "I made them happy and I made my dad proud. At the time that was all I really cared about."

"And how long did this go on for?" Matt kept his eyes on the road.

"Well, I guess until…that night. Till a few months before my eighth birthday." She swallowed loudly.

Matt made a face. "I'm sorry. You don't have to talk about this."

Shannon shook her head. "No, I want to tell you. I want to trust you." Matt nodded. "I never slept well," she began again. "So I shared a room with David. If I woke and got upset I just climbed into bed beside him and listened to his breathing. Some nights he woke too, some nights he slept on. On…that night, I woke at some ungodly hour of the morning and climbed in beside David. He didn't wake. For some reason I still couldn't settle and I got up again. I thought I might go and wake Sophie, or maybe Mummy and Daddy but I couldn't seem to make myself move from the foot of the bed. I stood for a long time looking at the closed door. I felt really, really afraid. The house was quiet, peaceful, but I just knew that I shouldn't leave the room. I managed to make myself walk over and put my hands on the door." In the car, Shannon put her hands up in front of her, palms forward, as though she was back in that night, her palms pressed against the warm wood of her bedroom door. Matt considered pulling over but she began talking again before he could make a decision. "I don't know why I did that or how long I sat like that but eventually my palms began to tingle, like pins and needles and I thought maybe I'd been sitting there too long. I was about to move when this weird sensation, like a mild electric shock maybe, went through them and I could taste blood on my tongue." In the car she was looking at her palms in wonder. "I woke David, shook him as hard as I could and by the time he was awake enough to listen to me, I knew what I was feeling. There was something in the house. Something or someone evil. David thought at first that I'd been dreaming and he was trying to persuade me to get back into bed when we heard a scream. I'll never forget it. My sister screamed only once but the terror in that sound made the hairs stand up on the back of my neck and brought my skin out in goose pimples" Listening to her talk, Matt was having the same reaction. He rolled his shoulders to get rid of the crawling sensation slipping down his spine." David and I looked at each other and I began to cry. And then my gorgeous, kind, funny, crazy, gentle big brother saved my life." Shannon stopped speaking for a moment and gulped back a sob.

Matt reached out and touched her arm. She smiled gratefully at him.

"There was a crawl space in our house. It led from room to room right around the whole structure. It was really small – just for pipes, ventilation and stuff but David pushed me in there and told me to crawl to the outside wall of the house, to stay there quiet as a mouse and not to come out until he told me to. I didn't want to go in, it was so claustrophobic and I didn't want to be alone without him. I begged him to come with me or let me stay but he kept on and on at me. A door banged down the hall, not to far from our room and I think I went beyond fear, I was absolutely terrified. I knew that something bad was coming. David gave me one last shove and pulled the panel shut behind me. It was under the bed on his side of the room and I could hear him moving things around but I didn't find out until later that he had gathered all his toys onto my bed to make it look as though no-one slept there."

"Smart boy," Matt remarked.

Shannon nodded. "Yes, yes he was. I'm not sure if he maybe intended to follow me in or if he already knew that it was too late. Maybe he hadn't thought beyond getting me out of that room. I don't know, but I waited for him until I heard the door to our room open. David made a noise, a kind of surprised grunt, there was a lot of movement, a scuffle I think, he screamed once and then there was silence. A terrible, heavy silence. I could feel that the man was standing in the middle of the room listening. I even imagined him sniffing the air. There were a few bangs and thumps in the room and I wanted to move but my body wouldn't obey my brain at all.

I heard the man leave the room, heard noises in other places in the house. I think he was looking for me. He really trashed the place, cleared out every closet and every other place he could find that was big enough for a child to hide in. It took a really long time and then I heard a car start in the garage and he left. He stole my dad's BMW convertible, took his keys from the key minder in the kitchen and just drove it away. It's never been found.

When my legs were finally able to move, I couldn't bring myself to go back into our bedroom. I didn't know what I'd find and I just couldn't find the strength to go through that panel again. I crawled to the end of the shaft, to the outside wall where David had told me to wait and I stayed there until sunlight began to filter through the cracks, then I crawled to mum and dad's room and got out."

Shannon put her shaking hands to her face and was surprised to feel the tears on her cheeks. Mitch had sat up in the back seat sometime during the story but he had kept silent. She drew a shaky breath and looked at Matt. "I'm sure you heard the rest on the news and in the papers. God knows every reporter in the universe seemed to be camped out on our driveway before I had even grasped what had really happened. Mum, dad and Sophie were in my parents' room. The bastard had shot mum and dad in the legs, bound and gagged them, then dragged Sophie in so they could watch while he raped her and slit her throat. Then he stabbed my mum eighteen times and finally, after making dad watch all that, finally he stabbed him in the throat so forcefully that he almost beheaded him. He had walked from room to room, checking all the closets on the way. He knew who was in the house, knew we would've heard Sophie scream, and knew that we'd hide."

Shannon swallowed. "I came out of the crawl space at the back of their en-suite and I could smell the blood. I dialled 911 and then called Greg, who was dad's superior at work. He was a lovely man, he always brought me chocolate." She smiled. "And then I sat down beside Sophie on the bed and waited."

She stopped talking and there was a sudden silence, emphasized by the drone of the car. "And David?" asked Matt.

Shannon smiled crookedly. "He wasn't in his room. There was no blood, nothing. He had just vanished. And he's never been found. I can't find him. No matter what I've tried, and believe me I've tried everything. I can see people who mean nothing to me; I can see what they're doing, where they are, who they're with. And my brother? Nothing. He saved my life and I can't feel anything when I touch his photo or hold his clothes. Nothing."

Shannon put her head in her hands and sobbed then, her body shaking as despair washed through her. Matt pulled over onto the hard shoulder and unbuckled his seat-belt but Mitch was faster. He leaned into the front seat and pulled Shannon into his arms, crooning softly to her as she shivered and cried. "I'm here," he was telling her. "I'm here, you're safe." Over Mitch's shoulder, Shannon's eyes met Matt's and he knew the story wasn't over.

Chapter Eleven

Mitch took over driving again and Matt spread himself out over the back seat and allowed his mind to drift, full of Shannon's story. He was getting a headache and the pain in his stomach was getting worse but it was bearable. He wondered for the thousandth time what exactly was going on. Someone was trying to get to Shannon, someone who, for whatever reason, had taken out her team first. That left her with no back-up, nothing but Mitch…his eyes sprung open and landed on Mitch, who was chatting to Shannon about what he fancied for a late dinner.

With no back up, Shannon had no-one to rely on but Mitch, or at least she hadn't until Matt had shown up. Was that why she'd been so insistent about bringing him along, even though he wasn't in great shape? Was that why she had found him a doctor? Why she so badly wanted to trust him? And the question now preying on Matt's mind led back home – why had Lewis sent him? He sighed and closed his eyes again. He needed to get Shannon alone for long enough to get some answers.

For now he was stuck with watching the back of her head as she stared out of the passenger window. Mitch was focused on the task of getting them into the city through three lanes of traffic. He whipped the car expertly from lane to lane, paying no attention to beeping horns and rude gestures.

"Where are we going?" asked Matt, leaning over to check road signs.

"Not far," Mitch told him. "Sean's to meet us on Amiens Street and direct us to a safe house somewhere. It would need to be close. I can't really risk being out on the streets here for too long."

The closer they got to Connolly Station, the slower the traffic seemed to move. It was after seven o'clock and the light had long since begun to fade but the area was still seething with people all hurrying in different directions. They stopped at traffic lights and a tide of people trooped across the road, native Dubliners clasping newspapers and bags of shopping, mixed with late holidaymakers dragging cases behind them and some back packers studying maps as they walked, the huge bags on their shoulders almost in danger of tipping them over backwards.

Mitch finally pulled the car in just above the North Star hotel and lit a cigarette as they waited.

It was almost an hour later when the mass of commuters leaving the station had slowed to a trickle that a man came staggering out from the road to their right. Dressed in filthy, baggy trousers and a threadbare hooded top he lurched from side to side spilling liberal amounts of a bottle that he carried in his left hand.

He crossed the road and walked towards the Hotel entrance, glancing back several times at the car. Matt watched him shrewdly but he wove his way on down the road, turning right towards the bar on the far corner, or perhaps the Centra shop. A few minutes later he staggered back around the corner, clutching a second bottle and trying to count money that he pulled from his pocket. Coins tinkled and rolled across the pavement as he walked and he cursed and muttered at them as they fell.

"Heads up," said Mitch, extinguishing his fourth or fifth cigarette.

Matt fingered the edge of his gun and waited. The tramp stopped beside the car, leered at Shannon, exposing a grimy face and yellow teeth. He leaned in past her, thrusting his dirty, alcohol soaked hand at Mitch and dropping a folded note into the waiting palm. "Spare a euro, man?" he questioned, the lilting Dublin accent almost lost in the harsh rasp.

"Christ, Sean, you stink!" Shannon wrinkled up her nose and pushed herself as far into her seat as she could. Mitch grinned and unfolded the small slip of paper, leaning forward and trying to catch his son's eye..

"Know the way?" Sean asked, his voice back to its normal timbre. Mitch nodded and opened his mouth to say something else but Sean was already reeling away, taking off back down the same road that he had emerged from.

Scowling faintly, Mitch started the car. "We'll detour around for a bit, I'll show you the sights. Ok there, Shan?"

She nodded, wrapped her arms around herself again and went

back to looking out the window as Mitch took them past Grafton Street, Trinity College, the Guinness Storehouse, the infamous General Post Office and the hugely impressive Custom House. Matt felt every inch the American tourist as he craned his neck to see to the glass pub at the top of the Guinness Storehouse but Shannon was quiet and withdrawn. Being on Mitch's turf didn't seem to agree with her.

Chapter Twelve

Mitch's Dublin was a maze of wide roads, narrow alleys and a never-ending sea of people hurrying up and down the foot paths or across the busy intersections. Horns blared and then slipped behind them as Mitch expertly navigated his way through the city, dodging taxis in the bus lanes and pedestrians in the road.

The grey stone of the city gradually gave way to red brick and Matt was aware of the sudden quiet as they travelled through the suburbs. Shannon was growing more anxious by the minute, her tense shoulders in the passenger seat the polar opposite of Mitch's relaxed and purposeful air. The tide had changed, Matt thought. Sometime between coming over the border and arriving in this city, Mitch had begun to celebrate whilst Shannon had begun to panic. He pressed his fingers to his temples where a headache was now raging. If they didn't get wherever they were going soon, he was going to have to give in and ask Shannon for some pain killers.

Mitch drove past the end of the cul-de-sac that they were looking for, barely glancing its way and swung the car down several more streets, keeping an eye in his mirrors as he finally doubled back and parked in the centre of a tree-lined avenue in front of a non-descript, two storey, red brick house which looked like all the others.

He turned off the engine and they sat quietly for a few moments listening to it cool down with a soft click, click, click. Matt was watching the road behind them; Mitch scanned the front, while Shannon kept an eye on the houses.

The street remained quiet, no curtains twitched, no lights went on or off in any windows, no cars turned into the street or left it. Mitch turned in his seat and nodded to Shannon and Matt, his dark eyes suddenly serious.

"Let's go," he said softly. "Quiet and quick. Watch your backs."

They left the car behind, carrying a bag each and covered the distance to the cul-de-sac in less than five minutes. Mitch stopped at the end of the street and glanced around. Shannon pulled her bag higher onto her shoulder and glanced back at Matt. He could see the tension in her mouth, the strain behind her eyes. He nodded at her, only a slight movement of his head. She frowned and Matt nodded towards Mitch, again the barest of movements. Shannon turned away from him, rolling her shoulders and taking a few deep breaths. Mitch motioned them into the garden of a house three doors down. All the windows in the house above were dark, the garden neat but devoid of colour. They took a side alley around the back of the house, pausing at the garden wall to listen for a few moments and then moving on through the next back garden where a square of light spilled from the kitchen over a patio.

The three of them skirted the edges of the light, eyes darting from window to window. Inside a young couple was eating supper, oblivious to their uninvited guests. Mitch kept watching them, a hand on the semi-automatic tucked into his shoulder holster, until Shannon and Matt were safely over the side wall. With a final glance behind him, Mitch swung himself over and dropped soundlessly beside the crouched forms waiting for him. He signalled to Matt that they had arrived at their destination and then crept past him to Shannon. He looked at her for a moment, right into her eyes. In the shadow of the wall, Shannon could see very little of his face but she could feel the pressure of his intense scrutiny. She waited. The moment passed and Mitch led them on.

They arrived at the back door of the house and flattened themselves against the red brick. Matt was sweating. His headache was back and his limbs were beginning to feel heavy and slow. He was breathing hard, almost gasping between breaths. Shannon glanced in his direction, frowning, looked away and then looked back again. She dropped her bag at her feet and put her free hand to his brow, winced and then brushed his hair back from his face a little. Matt leaned his head back. Her hand felt cool on his brow. He closed his eyes, almost moaning in protest when she took her hand away. Pulling the long fabric belt from the waistband of her jeans, Shannon hunkered down and wiped it across the grass which was wet from an earlier shower. Rising up again she pressed the old scarf to Matt's brow, then his face and his neck. She felt him lean gratefully against it.

Mitch had crept away towards the corner of the house, checking around the side alley and towards the front. Shannon watched as he slid around the corner of the house and was swallowed by the shadows, then she turned her attention back to Matt. Lifting his hand she pressed her fingers to his pulse and counted. It was strong but fast and she chewed on her lip. She dropped his hand and pressed her back against the wall again, checking for any sign of Mitch coming back.

Matt rolled his head around and opened his eyes. His head was almost on her shoulder.

"I feel like shit," he whispered.

Shannon shushed him but grinned. "We'll get you doped up again soon as Mitch's checked everything out and we can get inside." she whispered back.

Matt's eyes closed as he smiled. "Great," he managed to croak.

To his left the back door opened. Shannon was around him in a split second, gun drawn, blocking him with her body.

"Jaysus, Shannon! Don't shoot!" Sean held up his hands, palms wide. He was smiling broadly but Shannon kept the weapon trained on him as she reached back with her left arm and peeled Matt from the wall. He leaned on her, unsteady and took a moment to focus on the man blocking the door.

"Alright, Sean?" he asked, his voice shaking just a little.

Sean frowned and looked him up and down with a practiced eye and then shouted back into the house for help. Footsteps headed towards them and a light came on somewhere beyond the small back hall. Sean and Shannon kept their eyes on one another but said nothing.

"Bring him on in, Shan," said Mitch switching on a light just inside the door. It was a small bare bulb providing a small circle of meagre light. Mitch stepped forward and motioned her to follow him in.

Her eyes still on Sean, Shannon re-holstered the gun and then propped her shoulder under Matt's arm and half-carried him into the house. Sean watched them go and shut the door behind them.

Chapter Thirteen

The kitchen was large and warm with a red range in the corner and a large pine table in the centre of the room. There was an oversized saucepan bubbling on the range and the smells coming from it made Shannon's mouth water.

Sean followed her into the room and longed against the creamy coloured units on the far wall. A young woman stood up from her seat at the table, welding herself to his side and eyeing them all suspiciously. She was a few inches smaller than Shannon, with long red hair which fell in a tumble of wild curls all the way down her back. Her flashing green eyes caught sight of Matt and a smile of recognition quickly became a frown of concern.

"Is he still sick, then?" she asked, turning her porcelain doll features up to Sean.

Shannon pulled her bag off her shoulder and rummaged in it for medicine while Mitch busied himself helping Matt sit at the table.

"This here is Erin," Sean said proudly as the red head came to stand behind Matt, placing a palm on his forehead and wincing. Shannon was opening and closing cupboard doors. She finally located a glass and filled it with water then fed two pills to Matt and held the water to his lips.

Shannon caught Erin's eye over the top of Matt's head and Erin backed off, frowning. "I've made up three beds," Erin said gesturing to the door. "I wasn't sure what the sleeping arrangements would be." She looked from Shannon to Matt and then to Mitch. "I also made a good big pot of stew 'cause I knew you'd be hungered. Do you fancy a wee bowl, Matt?"

Sean shook his head. "Will you lay him alone, woman! Jaysus! They've been on the road for most of the day and the last thing they need is to listen to your shite." Erin rolled her eyes and resumed her seat at the table where a mug of steaming tea was waiting for her.

Mitch stepped up in front of Sean and, after a moment's hesitation, shook his son's hand. They were even more alike than

Matt had thought – same dark hair; same handsome, chiselled features; same dark blue eyes. Shannon took a seat beside Matt and watched the family reunion with narrowed lips.

Matt was soon feeling better, his splitting headache receded to a dull ache and he was able to join the others drinking tea that was strong enough to stand a spoon in and eating Erin's stew. It was delicious; warming him from the inside out – he had a second bowl which made Erin beam with pride and earned him a look of astonishment from Shannon.

The heat in the kitchen and his pleasantly full stomach had him yawning and struggling to keep his eyes open within the hour. Grinning at him, Erin suggested that he might like to check out his room and Shannon helped him to his feet. With a final, sleepy grin at Mitch and Sean, Matt allowed himself to be helped from the kitchen by the two women and fell asleep before his head hit the soft pillows of another borrowed bed.

Downstairs, Sean produced a bottle of Bushmills and poured two glasses. Mitch waited, accepting a glass with a smile and a nod. He took a few sips, grinning as Sean downed his in one gulp and poured himself another.

"Been a long time," Sean began, concentrating on his glass.

Mitch nodded and waited. He didn't want to rush this. Sean was working up to the hard questions – he would give him the time to do it his way.

"So, the whole name change thing," Sean said.

"Aye. I had to leave Michael Connor behind – he was a bit too popular for all the wrong reasons." Mitch leaned forward and motioned towards the bottle. Sean slid it over to him.

"But you still look like…yourself."

Mitch smiled. "I thought about changing that too but I was used to the guy that stared back at me from the mirror every morning so I figured the name change would have to do – I got all the papers to go with it, and the background."

"Does Mitch Cooper have a son?" Sean asked, his eyes glancing towards his father and then away again.

Mitch sighed. Now they were getting to it. "No. Mitch has

been married twice but he's never had children."

Sean nodded and there was an uncomfortable silence for a few minutes. Mitch bit his tongue.

"You were only in the North, it's not that far away. Or maybe you couldn't drag yourself away from your bit of stuff." Sean's face was carefully neutral but his eyes blazed.

"It wasn't like that, Sean," Mitch told him.

"The shite I had to listen to. From Mam, from the lads, from your so called pals. Did you never wonder what would happen to us when you disappeared from the universe and then turned up with a girl half your age?"

Mitch took a breath. "I didn't leave to find another woman, Sean. I left to give you a chance. If I'd stayed around, then we'd all be dead by now."

Sean slammed his glass onto the table and stood up, leaning across and pointing a finger into Mitch's face. "That's bollocks. You didn't do anything for us, you did it for you. The famous Michael Connor got scared and ran to save his own arse."

Mitch shook his head and took another sip of his whiskey. "Blade's a liar," he said calmly.

Sean frowned. "How did you…?"

"Blade would do anything to make me look bad. He's a back stabbing shite and he's been after your mother for years. You know that he can't be trusted or you wouldn't have lasted this long. Your mother's not daft either – she's bound to have told you to feed him just enough to keep him sweet but to handle the important stuff yourself."

Sean sat down. "So tell me."

"Tell you what?"

"What went on back then? Why you left. I think I'm old enough to handle it all now, don't you?"

Michael looked across the table at his son. Sean was almost 24 now and so like him that it made his breath catch. He imagined that Grace must've been highly pissed off when she realized that her son was the image of his father. "Your mother never told you?"

Sean shook his head. "She said that if I ever saw you again then I should ask – you should be the one to tell me."

Mitch raised his eyebrows. "And no-one else spilled the beans?"

Sean snorted. "They knew that Mam would take a baseball bat to their knee-caps if they did."

Mitch laughed. Yep, that sounded like Grace.

"So?" Sean sat back and folded his arms.

Mitch sighed and raked his fingers through his hair. He drained the last of the Bushmills. "I got involved with the lads at the grand old age of fourteen. Both my brothers were running weapons for them and for me, joining up was inevitable. I was just running errands mostly, a letter here and a pay-off there. Anyway, I got noticed by Padraig Kelly for whatever reason. He gave me a weapon, taught me how to shoot with it and sent me off to use it. I took to it like a duck to water. They told me who to shoot and I went and did it. It was like a game – cowboys and Indians with real people as the Indians and me as the lone ranger. The people down the scope were just targets and as soon as I pulled the trigger, I forgot that they'd ever existed. They started sending me further and further North, bedding me in until I was needed. And then one fine day I was approached by the UDA."

Sean's eyes widened. "Loyalists found you? Did you shoot them all?"

Mitch shook his head. "No. They wanted me to shoot someone. Said they'd pay me. So I did the job, got the money and…"

"Wait. You were working for both sides?"

Mitch sighed. "It was never about some glorious cause for me, Sean. It was about firing the gun, feeling the power. Getting paid for it just made it even better and I didn't give a shit who was bankrolling the job. I got approached by all kinds of organisations, from all these different countries and, since you didn't use your own name or give out personal details it was all easy. It was all exchanges of information – stuff was left at a hotel in a certain city. I went there, got the Intel, did the job, headed home. Payment was made to a P.O box in Sheffield and I paid winos to go and collect for me. I was making trips to England regularly for Kelly anyway."

"And Mam? Where did she fit in?"

"Aye your Mam." Mitch smiled into the past for a moment. "She was Padraig Kelly's grand-daughter so we got introduced a lot. She was proud, beautiful, strong-willed and she didn't take any shite from anyone. I married her when I was eighteen and you came along when I was twenty. By that stage I was already running my own black market deals and things went well for a good few years. I even took on a legit job – got into the Panthers although for ages I couldn't figure out how I'd passed the security clearance. I was a cocky wee shite, I suppose, thought I'd been really clever and fooled everyone." He looked up at Sean. "Turned out I was fooled."

"How?"

"Apparently the big cheese himself, Lewis Carter, was on my case and had cleared the way for me to get the job in the Panthers. We cut a deal – I got the slate wiped clean, a new identity and a wage in return for being a one man protection squad for an operative." Mitch paused.

"So there was a catch?" Sean prompted.

Mitch made a face. "The catch was my family. Carter had info that someone high up in Kelly's organisation was getting suspicious of my…activities. To be honest, I was surprised it had taken so long. Anyway, the word was that this person had gone to Padraig Kelly and he had already done the leg work, had found someone willing to take us out. Would've broken his heart to have his grand-daughter and great-grandson killed but he had to make an example of me, of us. He couldn't have the lower ranks thinking that he was turning into a soft auld granddad. If I agreed to the deal in its entirety then Carter agreed to remove the threat and your protection would be assured."

"Why couldn't we know? Why couldn't we go with you?"

"I couldn't take on Padraig Kelly and his organisation, Sean. At the time I didn't even know who the snitch was so I couldn't take him out either. And to take you with me would've meant that Kelly would've never rested until he found us. I made the agreement, didn't even pack a bag, just left."

Sean nodded. "Kelly was shot two days after you left - a clear sniper shot. He died instantly. A guy called Fergal McCaughan died in a car crash less than twenty-four hours later. His car was found to be full of bomb-making equipment and two silenced forty-fives. Carter had the reach to kill Kelly AND the guy he'd hired to take us out?"

Mitch nodded. His head ached with too much whiskey, too little sleep and too many memories. "I need to hit the hay, Sean. I'm sure you need to think about what's going on here. We'll talk again tomorrow." He stood up and headed for the door.

"Who was it?" asked Sean, his voice steady. Mitch grimaced. "The snitch, who was it?"

"I don't know," Mitch answered him, keeping his hand on the handle of the door and his back to his son.

"You said that you didn't know back then but I'm willing to bet that you found out, made it your business to find out. That's what I would've done. Who was it?"

"Sean, it's not a good idea to…"

Sean stood up, his chair bouncing onto the floor behind him. Mitch whirled to face him as his son grabbed him by the front of his shirt and pushed him back against the door. Mitch grunted as the small of his back connected with the door handle.

"Don't you fuckin' lecture me," Sean hissed. "You have no right. You owe me this much, you piece of shit. Now. Who. Was. It?"

Mitch stared into Sean's eyes for a moment. Sean was shaking, anger spilling over into his eyes. He pushed against Mitch's windpipe again. "You sure you want to know this?" asked Mitch softly. Sean nodded. "Promise me you'll not act on this, Sean."

Sean shook his head. "No. Unlike you, I don't make promises that I can't keep."

Mitch sighed. "It was Blade." He moved quickly, his hands rising in a blur of movement and then chopping down to remove Sean's hands from the front of his shirt, even as he dropped down and snapped the flat of his hand against Sean's solar plexus. Winded, Sean flew backwards crashing into and then over his fallen chair.

Mitch adjusted his shirt and looked down at his gasping son. "Don't try a move like that on me again."

Sean lay on the floor until his breathing was back to normal and Mitch's footfalls on the stairs had drifted away. It made sense – Blade was a liar, Mitch was right about that. He was also ambitious, ruthless and getting to an age when he was running out of time to fulfil his ambitions. Sean wondered if leading the organisation was on Blade's list of things-to-do-before-I-die. He'd have to talk to Grace.

Pulling himself off the floor, Sean righted the chair and rinsed the glasses in the sink, setting them carefully on the draining board. Erin could be a right cow about things not being left tidy.

Giving the room a final glance, Sean switched off the light and headed to bed.

Chapter Fourteen

Matt woke the next morning to the sounds of a busy house. Sticking his head out of his bedroom door, he spotted Erin and asked her what was going on.

"The powers that be wanted a demo and Grace managed to arrange something for our girl to show off with. Hope she's as good as you all say she is. Sean's arranging transport to Ballystewart. You well enough to tag along?"

Matt was washed and dressed exactly eight minutes later. He still needed a shave and a haircut but at least he was showered and dressed in clean clothes. Shannon grinned at him as he came into the kitchen. "Clean again?" she asked.

"Squeaky," he answered, accepting a strong coffee and a plate of toast from Erin. He nodded his thanks to her and sat down at the table beside Shannon to eat.

Mitch was pacing the room, listening to Sean as he called in favour after favour to get them the twenty miles to Ballystewart without anyone finding out who they were and what they were doing. Mitch's face was grim and there were dark circles under his eyes.

"How's the head this morning?" Shannon asked in a whisper.

"Delicate," Matt told her around a mouthful of toast. "Feels like the morning after a really good night out."

They grinned at each other.

"We got many of those magic pills left?" He asked.

Shannon shook her head. "Not many but we can get more if we need them."

"You know a lot of useful people?" Matt asked.

Shannon glanced at Mitch. "I hope so." She whispered before rising from the table and rinsing her cup at the sink.

One hour later they were on their way in a dark blue Mondeo estate driven by Erin. Shannon sat beside her staring out the window and fiddling with her rings and bracelet. Matt, Mitch and Sean were squeezed into the back seat with Mitch heavily disguised in a blonde wig and matching moustache. Matt thought he looked like Butch Cassidy, or was it the Sundance kid? Or maybe he looked like a weird mixture of the two. Whatever, he didn't make the mistake of telling Mitch his thoughts.

The trip lasted thirty minutes thanks to the heavy traffic and the conversation was muted and confined to the mild weather for the time of year and the ingredients of Erin's stew. Matt was delighted when Erin pointed out the sign at the entrance to the village and a few seconds later they spotted a Garda officer leaning against an unmarked police car.

"Pull in," said Sean. "Matt, Erin, you two stay in the car. Shannon, Da…er, I mean, Mitch, you come with me. Let me do the talking."

Erin swung the car in behind the Garda and began chewing on her nails as Mitch, Shannon and Sean got out. Matt looked around. No sign of anyone watching or hiding. They were in a wide open area with few hiding places apart from some tubs brimming with flowers. Matt was inclined to think that the village was gearing up to enter one of those 'In Bloom' competitions – everything looked clean and tidy, colourful and well-tended.

"He fancies her y'know," mumbled Erin. She had folded her arms sullenly and was watching Shannon shake hands with the Garda while Sean talked and Mitch stood watching.

"Who? Mitch?" Matt leaned over a little to get a better view through the windscreen.

"No." Erin sounded disgusted. "Sean. He told me so this morning – thinks she's well fit, loves her accent, thinks she has lovely skin and beautiful eyes." She made a harrumph sound. "I don't trust her. She likes to play games, that one. Keep you all hanging while she messes with your heads and makes you crazy. I've known girls like her – pretty girls who know that they're pretty and use their looks to get men to do what they want. She's been turning on the charm with Sean to get him to introduce her to the right people then she'll piss off back to whatever shit hole she crawled out of and he'll come running back to me with his tail between his legs and that stupid wounded puppy look on his face. She's already got Mitch dancing to her tune but I suppose he can only take her so far. She's bored with him and looking to move on to her next man. Look at him. He's almost drooling over her."

Matt looked. "Who? Sean?" Sean was turned away from Shannon, talking to the Guard who looked none too happy.

Erin tsked and looked at him over her left shoulder. "No, Mitch."

Matt made a face and looked back. Shannon was standing by herself a little way between Mitch and Sean, her eyes on the ground and her arms wrapped around herself. "Erin, I don't think Shannon has any interest in Sean. She's been friendly to him, yes, but only because you two're putting us up. Maybe she just doesn't know the difference between being friendly and flirting."

Erin scowled. "Oh, she knows the difference alright. Sounds to me like she has you all fooled. Know why?"

Matt shook his head, amused and concerned all at once.

"'Cause you're all bloody men, that's why. Thinkin' with your dicks instead of your heads." Erin sighed. "I should phone Grace, tell her what a mess this is. Grace wouldn't put up with some silly American bitch turning her son's head away from business."

Matt shook his head. "Phone her then." He sat back and folded his arms. "Just remember who Sean works with. You know how they all feel about Michael Connor. How would they all feel if they knew Sean was hiding a traitor? Would they give him the benefit of the doubt? Give him a chance to explain it all?" Erin looked away and Matt sat forward again, leaning into the front of the car and turning her to face him. "They'd shoot him in the head, Erin."

Erin narrowed her eyes at him. "You seem to think you know a lot about us."

Matt nodded. "I learned a lot last time." He sighed. "Look, Erin, Shannon isn't going to take Sean away from you and Sean isn't really interested in Shannon – she's a part of his Dad's life and that makes her exotic. He's curious about her. I mean, she kept his Dad up North for the past twelve years, kept him away from his son and his past. That makes her dangerous and, well, maybe an enemy." They both looked towards the quartet who were shaking hands and heading back to the car. "Sean loves you and he loves his Mum. Some dolly bird with long legs and pretty eyes isn't going to change that."

Erin opened her mouth to reply but Mitch was already opening the back door. Matt looked up at him. "Everything okay?"

Mitch nodded. "Yeah. The guy's a tough negotiator but we're in."

Shannon and Sean climbed back into the car.

"We've got directions to the house," Mitch was saying. "It's just past the Chapel, set back from the road and detached which suits us very well. The neighbours and Gardai are pretty much camped out at it but there's a back lane which our boy, Nathan, is covering. He'll get Shannon in. Erin, can you drive as far back as Ferguson's Corner? Know it?" Erin nodded. "You can all wait there and when we're done, I'll call you to come and pick us up."

"No," Said Shannon and everyone turned to look at her. "I want Matt with me."

Mitch's eyes narrowed and there was an uncomfortable silence in the car. Matt felt Erin's cool gaze on him. See, she was signalling with her eyes, I told you she likes to play games.

Mitch turned to Matt and his face was impassive. "I'll fill you in on the way."

Matt nodded and sat back as Erin pulled away from the side of the road and headed for the East of the town. Mitch pulled a cell phone from his inside pocket and handed it to Matt.

"It's a clean phone with one pre-programmed number – mine. We'll drop you off about half-way up the lane behind the houses. Nathan, the Garda will be waiting and he'll show you in. The parents are expecting you and know that this is a strictly behind the door affair. They're willing to take the chance anyway. At least the mother is. Shannon will know what to do and how to do it. You just have to follow her lead, support her if she needs it and call me when she's done. We'll meet you at the far end of the lane. Any questions?"

Matt turned the phone over in his hands, switched it on and checked the battery and the speed dial, then slotted it into the pocket of his jacket. "Just one," he said, "What the hell is going on?" No-one answered him and Matt sighed. Information on this outing was obviously on a need-to-know basis and the powers that be, Mitch and Sean, seemed to have decided to keep him out of the loop.

Erin slowed the car and they all glanced out of the windows. They were turning onto a dirt track behind a row of about eight fairly large, detached bungalows. They bumped up the track for a few feet.

"Stop here." Shannon said. "We can walk from here. It'll give me time to explain things to Matt." She climbed out of the car and Matt followed her, closing the door softly behind him and not looking back – he knew that all he would see would be Mitch, Sean and Erin glaring after them.

They walked a few paces and then Matt stopped. "Tell me." He said.

Shannon made a tutting noise and pulled his arm. "Keep walking you idiot. We won't get a chance to talk properly if you mess this up."

Matt raised an eyebrow but did as he was told.

" I've waited for a long time to have someone on my side in this mess and I hope to hell it's you. Otherwise I'm screwed." She looked at him for his reaction.

Matt frowned. "I'm not sure what any part of this whole situation is, Shannon and I definitely don't have a clue what my part in it is supposed to be so why don't you start from the beginning."

"There isn't time. I'm going to have to go through this quickly and hope you get it. Mitch has been looking after me ever since I was eighteen. Your father assigned him to me and set things up so that I could try to have a decent life. I wasn't off the payroll but it was as close as I was going to get. I thought he was one of the most attractive men I'd ever met and he had a lot of charm but he was my bodyguard and I figured he was off limits."

"Knowing Mitch he was able to change that point of view pretty fast," Matt said softly.

Shannon nodded, her face down. "We became…lovers… shortly after my twenty-second birthday and I adored him for a long time." Matt shrugged uneasily. "Look, I'm telling you this so that you understand why I was maybe a little too slow to figure out what was happening until it was too late." Shannon whispered fiercely.

"The jobs kept coming and I did them as I always did – it was a clever set-up. None of us ever got to know anyone's identity and Mitch took care of all the in between stuff while I did the job, warmed his bed, drank some wine, played some music and kept my head in the sand about the details. I didn't have to worry about it, y'know? Not even money. He gave me an allowance, just like a child, bought me lots of stuff too."

"He had access to your money?" Matt was surprised. His father would never have set things up that way.

"My trust fund is accessible only to me but I've never had to use it. The day I turned eighteen your father took me to the bank and I withdrew three million dollars."

"Whew."

"Mmmm. I didn't know what to do with it so naturally I turned to Mitch for advice. He took it and I only found out recently what happened to it."

"Do I want to know?" Matt grimaced.

"It was deposited in four separate bank accounts under the names of several of Michael Connor's past associates. They skim a percentage every month in return for the use of their names. When money is needed, Mitch contacts a go-between who contacts the associates and the money is transferred between us all with people taking their cuts left right and centre. The house in Portstewart was the only thing that your father managed to arrange for me. It's in my great, great, great grandmother's maiden name with wills changed to name me as sole heir to my family's three homes." She grinned at Matt's raised eyebrow. "C'mon, Matt you know that you can get anything done for the right amount of cash." She shook her head. "We're getting off the point. So one night, Mitch sat me down and told me that he had some bad news – Lewis was retiring and was looking for a nest egg – he had double crossed us and was trying to sell me."

"Sell you?" Matt was incredulous.

"You remember how I said I had always felt like just another commodity. Well, Mitch knew how I felt; he was clever and knew exactly how to use my insecurities. Mitch said that we should be very careful about trusting Lewis Carter or any of the operations teams from now on. He thought it would be best if we changed the rules a bit, let men that he trusted liaise with the powers that be when jobs came down the line – the less contact we had, the better."

"And because you were in love with him, you trusted his judgement." Matt said gently. Shannon nodded. "So, how did you find out?"

She sighed. They were almost at the back of the fourth house, the place they were aiming for. "I explained to you about my gift." Matt nodded. Shannon was turned towards him, her eyes shadowed with anxiety. "I work very hard not to use it all the time. Not to read every single thing that I touch. It takes effort and concentration so I run a lot, I listen to music a lot. I try very hard to keep my distance from people if I can. To search someone's memories like that is an invasion of their privacy, almost a rape."

"But you read Mitch."

She nodded. "Little seeds of doubt crept into my mind. I can't explain it but it's like a feeling that something just isn't quite right. Do you know what I mean?" Matt nodded. "So yes, I seduced him, got him comfortable and one day when he went out to 'take care of business' I held one of his belongings and, kind of followed him." She looked away from him. The Garda was just ahead, watching them carefully and glancing back at the house nervously. "I think we need to go."

"I take it that it was worth it?" Matt asked sharply.

Shannon looked at him, surprised by his tone. "What do you mean?"

"Whoring yourself. You got the information you wanted?" Matt bit his tongue, not really certain who he was angry at or why.

Shannon swallowed and blushed. She looked at him sadly. "It wasn't like that, Matt, it was…," she sighed. " Look - Mitch was lying. He was the one who was selling me, to his old friends who I understand are going to use me to help them target the people who can damage them and their organization. Maybe even more than that. Mitch is a git, but a clever one." She waved to Nathan and together they walked forward.

Matt's mind was jumbled. He felt like he should apologise or at least have something deep and meaningful to say about the fact that someone she had trusted was trying to 'sell' her but he just couldn't get his brain to move beyond the reality of Mitch and Shannon together. He changed the subject instead. "So what are we doing here?" he asked.

Shannon nodded to Nathan and they followed him into the back garden of the house. There was a swing set, a trampoline and a small sand pit. "There's a child missing from this house," Shannon whispered, glad of the change of subject. She reached out and touched the swings, closed her eyes briefly and sighed. "I'm going to try and find her. I want you to see what I do."

Matt frowned. An image of Charlene came into his head. He remembered his arms tightening around her when he realised that she was dying. He had held her little body tight against his chest and inhaled the scent of her – pineapple shampoo, strawberry toothpaste and that unique little girl scent of sunshine and fresh air. For a brief second, standing there in the back garden of an unfamiliar house in an unfamiliar corner of Ireland, he remembered the tickle of her hair against his lips as he kissed his daughter goodbye. Matt shivered, his breath caught in his throat and tears stung his eyes. Shannon looked back at him and her eyes filled with compassion. "I don't think I can…" Matt began. The words stuck in his throat and he swallowed.

Shannon nodded. "You can. You've lost a child, Matt, so you have an immediate connection with these people. You know the hurt, the anger and the helplessness that they must be going through right now. I can help them."

Matt nodded, his heart was thumping hard against his rib cage and he took several deep breaths to calm himself down. Nathan signalled for them to stop at the back door while he went inside. They waited in silence until the back door opened again and a small, blonde woman beckoned them in. Her eyes were red and puffy and her un-brushed hair had sprung up like a halo around her head. She was shaking as she closed the door behind them and put a finger to her lips.

They followed her down a short corridor and into a tiny office room. She closed the door softly and then turned to them. "I'm Sadie Lynch. Nathan said you'd asked for a quiet room and something that belonged…belongs to my child."

She bit her lip on a sob and Shannon leaned over and took her hand. "I'm Shannon, Sadie. I'm going to find your daughter and I'll be honest with you every step of the way. I'll tell you everything that I see, feel and hear. I won't hold anything back and it might be difficult for you to listen to. If you're going to have a problem with that then it might be best for you not to be in the room." She gestured to Nathan. "The Gard will be making a note of everything anyway."

Sadie shook her head and made an effort to keep control of herself. "No, I'd like to stay. I want to know where my baby is."

Shannon nodded and took a seat at the desk which was clear of everything but a Winnie The Pooh scarf. Sadie, Matt and Nathan pulled seats close and sat down too. Shannon pointed to Matt. "Sadie this is my friend Matt. He knows what you're going through."

Sadie turned to Matt. "Did Shannon find your child?"

Matt swallowed the painful lump in his throat. He glanced at Shannon who smiled encouragingly at him. Matt turned his full attention to Sadie. Her blue eyes, ringed with red and underscored with dark circles, were looking back at him in pained confusion. "My daughter Charlene was ten when our car was blown up by people who wanted to kill me. My wife was sitting beside me and was killed outright. I was thrown clear." He took a breath. "I crawled back to the car and pulled Charlene from it. She was alive but only just and I gave her CPR for as long as I could but there was no response and so I held her in my arms while she passed away. She was so young, so pretty, her whole life was in front of her." He paused, unsure if he was saying too much.

Sadie's eyes brimmed with tears and, as he spoke, one rolled down her face. "I'm sorry for your loss, Matt. My baby's been gone for almost 30 hours and I want her back. They've prepared me for the worst, y'know - that she might be...dead. If she is then I'm not sure how to deal with it but at least I'll know. If we never find her, never know...well, that would send me mad." She turned to Shannon. "How did you know?" she asked. "We were under strict instructions not to mention the gender."

Shannon smiled. "It's how my gift works, Sadie. I touched the swing on the way past and I felt her. Usually I just get an image of where the person is and what they're doing but sometimes I get other information too. She plays there with her little brother a lot and perhaps with her cousins when they visit. Her brother's presence is strong – he's in the house but she isn't."

Sadie sighed, her eyes wide and a new expression on her face. Matt recognized it at once – hope. He crossed his fingers that Shannon would be able to find the child – leaving this woman in any other circumstances would feel like a betrayal.

Shannon nodded and Nathan pulled out a notebook and pencil. Taking a deep breath, Shannon leaned forward and lifted the scarf, running it through her hands over and over. Matt watched carefully as her eyes glazed over and she relaxed back into her chair, his hand covered Sadie's where it rested on the table. Shannon's face relaxed, all life and expression left it. Her eyes stared at the table in front and Matt felt a chill slide across his shoulder blades.

****

Shannon tuned out the room and concentrated on the feel of the scarf running through her fingers, the softness of the yarn, the little pull near the far end where it had caught on the fence last winter, a small thread that would begin to unravel before Easter.

There was a label stitched under the fringed end with the care instructions on it, she could smell Anais Anais and knew that the perfume had been a gift from Granny Nelson for the child's twelfth birthday. She saw the child, Shauna she was called, spray it delightedly all around her room. There was the face of a boy called Oran Cassidy, Shauna had a major crush on him, giggled about him with her best friend who was called…Lesley…and was supposed to be going to the cinema in Rosslairn with him at the weekend. The scarf was childish but Shauna knew her mother had bought if for her and wore it to please her, putting up with the teasing of her friends because she loved her mother so much.

Bracing herself, Shannon lifted the scarf to her face, closed her eyes and inhaled deeply. She was immediately assaulted by images of the girl – small like her mother with those same clear blue eyes and short blonde hair. No freckles, just pale clear skin and a figure that was just beginning to gain womanly curves. Image after image flashed in Shannon's head and she sifted through them, searching for the recent past or the here and now. There were birthday parties, new jeans, dresses and frilly shirts giving way to tighter tops and hidden make-up, a puff of a cigarette on the way home from school, a taste of alcohol after a church disco and then there it was – a car and a rush of fear.

"Dark blue, five door Opel…something," Shannon began to speak in a clear but expressionless voice and Nathan immediately began taking notes. Shannon's head moved. She was in a memory, watching the car pass, slowing down, break lights coming on. "Licence is 95D33091. Man driving. Tall man, almost bald, just wisps' of grey hair. In his fifties maybe? Grey eyes, navy blue acrylic trousers, red shirt, stone jacket. She recognizes him. He's smiling. Safe to take a lift with him. We know him." Shannon shook her head. "No, Shauna, there's a knife in his pocket."

Sadie moaned, low in her throat and gulped back a sob. Matt reached out to squeeze her hand and she shivered then turned her attention back to Shannon who was now speaking in clipped tones, faster and faster. Nathan was scribbling furiously. "Can you get a name for this guy?" He asked but Shannon was speaking again.

"He watched her a lot. All started ages ago. He fought the urge but it all got too much and he came for her. Drove around her usual haunts until he found her. There's a cottage. It's on a river… no, wait, not a river it's the sea."She inhaled deeply. "I smell the sea weed and there's a lane…short lane, small cottage. Belongs to his family. Winding road nearby, sheep farm to the North. There's a gate at the farm, Higgins. Name on the gate is Higgins. He walks here a lot, likes the roar of the sea in a storm, and likes the isolation, perfect place to bring her…" she shook her head. "This is no good I need to go back." She concentrated and followed the dirt track away from the farm again and back towards the ocean. The cottage was almost hidden behind a hill just before the narrow stretch of beach. Shannon's mind reached out for Shauna's and then she was inside the cottage.

The man was there, watching something on a small black and white television. He was drinking beer and smoking a cigarette – his head was wreathed in a halo of smoke and he coughed hard as he laughed at something on the screen. There was a handgun on the arm of his chair and a rifle was propped up against the TV table. Shannon moved away from him and into another room. It was a kitchen, small, with no fridge but a lot of tins and a camping stove. There was an ancient sink in one corner and a few days' worth of plates and cups were piled up. A shotgun was bolted to the wall above a tiny, grime encrusted window. Shannon backed away again and into the cottage's only other room. She sighed. "She's here."

Shauna was lying on the bed, hands tied behind her back with several black cable ties. Her legs were tied at the ankles and knees with some kind of black wire or tubing, her jeans and Diesel top were filthy and the top was ripped at the shoulder. Her eyes were closed. Shannon moved closer, saw her chest rise and fall.

"She's alive but he's getting drunk. Get moving Nathan. I'll direct you by phone. Call for backup. He's got guns but you can take him – no lights, no sirens, surprise him and then take him down."

Nathan was gone, his chair tipping over in his wake. Shannon opened her eyes and looked across the small table towards Sadie. "She's alive, Sadie but she's scared. I need a nickname or something. Some way that she'd know her mum."

Sadie was crying silently, her fingers twisting and curling around each other in the agony of being unable to do anything but wait. "She's my little pixie; I call her 'Tink' to annoy her."

Shannon grinned and then closed her eyes again, sinking into herself and away from the warm room, Matt's anxious eyes and Sadie's silent pleas. She sent herself back to the bedroom of the cottage, gave herself a moment to gather some energy and then she spoke to Shauna.

Wake up Tink. I need your help. Wake up NOW.

Shauna's eyes popped open immediately and she glanced around. The voice had seemed to fill the whole room but there was no-one here. The only noise now was the muffled sound of the television, punctuated by his laughter. She could have sworn… Shauna sighed and laid her head back down.

I need his name, Shauna. We're coming for you but I want to be able to give the Gardai a name. It'll help us to find you.

Shauna frowned and struggled into a sitting position. She watched the door. If the voice had been as loud as it had seemed then he would be coming in. A few seconds ticked by and she heard the pop-fizz of him opening another can of beer. She cocked her head to the side, trying to ignore her cramping muscles, stinging cuts and tender bruises. Was she losing her mind?

I'm here, Shauna. I'm here with your mum. She wants her Tink back and there are people coming to get you but I need a name.

Shauna wet her lips and felt tears threaten for what seemed to be the millionth time. She wanted so much to believe that someone was coming and that she'd see her mum again. She thought about the man in the other room, of the things he'd sat here on this bed and told her that he'd do to her, of the way his tongue had licked his lips as he'd looked down at her.

"Davey," she whispered. "Davey McCarron."

"Davey McCarron," echoed Shannon inside the room at

Shauna's home.

"Sadie's hand flew to her mouth. "No!" she said, shaking her head, her eyes wild. "He rents from us every year, a quiet man, his wife left him and he..."

"Rents what?" Matt was on his feet, flipping open Michael's phone.

"A cabin just outside of the Skerries. He's a gentle, sweet man, joined us for dinner a few times, played out back with the kids last year. Took me into town for my messages. He couldn't. He just wouldn't. I can't...." Sadie put her face in her hands and sobbed.

Matt had dialled the number that Nathan had slipped to him and spoken to the Garda. They were on their way, driving at speed by the sound of it and Nathan was pumped up and ready for action. Matt closed the phone and laid a hand on Sadie's quivering shoulder. He glanced back at Shannon – she hadn't moved, was still sitting at the table with her eyes closed and the scarf in her hands. She was whispering.

In the cottage Shauna listened to the voice. *Gardai on their way, stall him if he comes in.*

Has he touched you?

Shauna shook her head but fingered the cuts and bruises from fighting against him when she realised that he wasn't taking her home.

Be brave, Tink. Just a little while longer and you'll be safe and back home with your mum and Dad. I won't leave you, I'm right here.

Shauna looked around and saw nothing but she didn't care. Imagining a guardian angel hovering above her was a comfort, even if it was just her mind playing tricks. She twisted on the bed; trying to bring some feeling back into her arms and legs in case she had to fight again. She paused. Something was different and it took her a few seconds to figure out what it was – there was quiet in the cottage. He had switched off the television. As though he'd been standing outside the room waiting for her to notice, Davey McCarron slowly opened the bedroom door and staggered in, beer in one hand. He closed the door behind him, set the beer down on the bedside table and smiled obscenely at Shauna, sliding a long silver object from his pocket. Still smiling, he sat down on the end of the bed and held it up for her to see. The blade slid out of its sheath with a whisper and, inside her head, Shauna began to scream.

****

Shannon grasped Matt's arm and asked for Nathan. She kept her eyes closed. Matt dialled the number and placed the phone to her ear. Shannon was following the lane from the cottage back to the closest intersection. She gave him directions in as much detail as she could. It was good news; they were closer than she'd thought – maybe ten minutes from the farmhouse. Shannon sighed and was just closing the connection when Shauna's scream reverberated in her head. Shannon dropped the phone and it bounced along the table as she threw her hands over her ears in agony. Matt and Sadie leapt to their feet.

"What's wrong with her? What's going on?" asked Sadie frantically. "It's Shauna, isn't it? What is it? What's happened to my baby?" She screamed the last question at Shannon who moaned and pushed herself back to a sitting position.

Matt had an arm around Sadie and was talking to her in hushed tones to calm her down when the door to the room opened and a ruddy faced man with strawberry blond hair and eyes that were full of anger and sorrow stepped in. He pulled Sadie into his arms, looked accusingly at Shannon and Matt and then dragged his wife from the room.

Matt sighed as the door closed. He pulled a chair close to Shannon who was shaking a little. She was whispering to herself, describing the scene inside the cottage as it unfolded. Matt shivered and listened.

McCarron had cut the ties on Shauna's ankles and knees, running the blunt edge of the knife along her thigh. He moved around and slipped the blade inside the hem of her jeans, slicing up the outside seam in a long, slow arc. Shauna whimpered and wriggled back a little. She had begun to shake. McCarron licked his lips and smiled at her, taking her hands in one of his.

"Calm down now pretty thing. Wouldn't want me knife to slip and draw blood now would we?" He chuckled and sliced through the cable ties around her wrists.

Shauna's mind was racing – she couldn't be here, this wasn't real. She was supposed to be going to the cinema with Oran this weekend not stuck in a dirty room getting sliced to bits by a lunatic. Her thoughts tumbled over one another – her mother kissing her forehead at bedtime, smelling of fresh soap and talcum powder. Her dad coming in from work, his boiler suit covered in oil and grease, smelling of old cars and leather seats. McCarron leaned forward to kiss her neck, his tongue sliding across her skin and leaving a snail trail of saliva that made Shauna gag.

She looked at the peeling paint on the ceiling, the dark stain in the corner where damp was making itself at home, the layer of dirt and dust on the windows, the yellowing curtains and, slowly, Shauna felt herself grow numb. She could feel McCarron's questing mouth with a kind of embarrassed detachment as her mind wandered and her gaze fell on the farthest corner of the room. In the deep shadows something moved and Shauna's eyes widened. A woman stood there. A tall woman who seemed to be made of shadow – insubstantial but becoming more real with each passing second. The woman's eyes glittered as she watched McCarron with a mixture of revulsion and anger. She walked forward, out of the corner and Shauna caught her breath. If this was her angel then she was an avenging angel. The woman caught Shauna's eye and raised a finger to her mouth.

Ssssssh, Shauna. Don't let him see me yet. I'm your little secret.

Shauna closed her eyes, squeezed them tight and then opened them again. The woman was still there, clearer now – tall and lithe with high cheekbones, large grey eyes fringed by long lashes, a full mouth with generous Angelina Jolie lips and long dark hair that cascaded over her shoulders and swung down to her hips. Her eyes were on McCarron as she slipped across the room to stand just behind his left shoulder.

Close your eyes, Tink. This'll all soon be over.

Shauna swallowed as McCarron's hand danced along the curve of her breast and then she closed her eyes and waited.

Davey McCarron lifted his head and frowned. He'd felt strange for just a moment – like someone was watching him. Sitting back on the small bed, he shuddered.

Back at the Lynch's home, Matt was watching Shannon anxiously. Her breathing was regular and slow but her pallor had grown more and more ghostly. She suddenly took a deep breath and whispered fiercely "Oh, no, no, no. I will not let you."

Matt chewed his lip and swung back on his chair. He wished he knew exactly what was going on, wished he was in the middle of it all out there at that cottage or sitting at home in front of the late show with a beer and microwave popcorn – anything but sitting here unable to help. He rubbed his eyes, closing them for a moment to calm himself again and then he looked back at Shannon and got the shock of his life. Shannon was there but her image was wavering – an outline with transparent shading as she raised a finger to her lips and smiled at someone he couldn't see.

Matt stood up and backed away a little, his heart was hammering in his chest and his eyes were wide and fixed on her. The air around her seemed to shimmer and then she was back, pale and shaking as she grasped the edge of the table. She looked up at him and then grimaced in pain, putting her fingers to her temples.

"Shannon…?" Matt gasped, searching for something to say.

Somewhere in the house a phone rang and was answered as they faced each other across the small room. Beyond the door there was a whoop of delight and someone shouted "They've got her, she's safe. Where's Sadie?"

Shannon pulled herself to her feet and almost slid to the floor again. Her legs were like jelly and her head was filled with a hot white pain. Matt was beside her in seconds, his arm around her waist as he helped her stand.

"We have maybe twenty minutes before I pass out, Matt. I

don't usually do that but he was going to.... You have to get me out before...." Her voice trailed away as she gripped her head in both hands. Matt began walking her to the door. "Phone. Get them here." She gasped as another lance of pain shot through her.

Matt opened Mitch's phone and hit the speed dial. "We've got trouble. Bottom of the hill below the bungalows in ten minutes." He closed it again and opened the door.

The house was in chaos – people were crying, laughing, running around. Kettles were being boiled and calls to the rest of the family and friends were being made. Matt and Shannon slipped back the way they had come and back down the lane with Matt half carrying, half dragging her all the way.

"Matt," Shannon whispered, her chin dipping onto her chest.

Matt paused and leaned close to her. "What is it, Shannon?"

"Mitch...don't tell him. He mustn't know what I can do."

"What did you do?"

Shannon lifted her head and gasped at the flash of agony behind her eyes. She managed a weak smile at Matt. "I sent myself to the cottage and when he saw me he had a heart attack."

"Davey McCarron?" She nodded and her head fell forward again. "Wait. What do you mean you 'sent' yourself there?"

There was no answer. Shannon had passed out. Matt adjusted her weight and reached down under her knees, lifting her fully into his arms. Her head fell back and he lifted her up a little higher so that it rested on his shoulder. He walked to the bottom of the lane as fast as he could, sighing with relief when Erin swung the car around in front of him. Mitch and Sean leapt from the car, concern on both their faces. "Did she find the kid?" Sean asked.

Matt nodded as Mitch touched a gentle hand to Shannon's face. "What the hell happened?" He asked, his voice low and hard.

Matt shook his head. "I dunno. It seemed to take a lot out of her." He looked Mitch in the eye. "I thought maybe this was normal."

Mitch shook his head. "Normal? Jesus, Matt. Here, let's get her into the back. I'll go in the far side and you can reach her in."

Within minutes they were racing away back to the city with

Shannon lying across their knees, cradled into the crook of Matt's arm. Her head lifted once as they drove and she looked around groggily.

"Quite a night," Matt said softly.

"Yeah? You're a cheap date, Carter. Never would've guessed."

Matt grinned. "Ah, you never said it was a date. If I'd known I'd have had a shave, got a haircut, worn a suit…"

She sighed. "Bullshit. You've been promising that for weeks." She drifted off again and Matt sighed, leaned his head back and closed his eyes. He could feel Mitch watching him and imagined that he would have a lot of questions to answer once they got back.

Chapter Fifteen

The house seemed deserted. Shannon poured herself a coffee and sat down at the kitchen table. Her head still hurt but it was a dull ache this morning, not the lancing pain of the past few days. She sighed and rolled the bitter brew around her mouth. If she was to do that again, she would need a month to recover.

The kitchen door opened and Mitch came in, smiling as he saw her. "Morning, princess. Feeling better?"

Shannon nodded. "Much." She raised her mug. "Coffee helps."

Mitch laughed. "Grace used to say that coffee and chocolate were two of man's greatest inventions."

Shannon nodded. "And she was right."

Mitch busied himself with making more coffee – grinding beans, changing the filter, measuring the correct water level. Shannon waited, knowing that his activities were a cover – what he really wanted to do was sit down and interrogate her. Eventually, coffee made, Mitch poured a cup and leaned against the counter. "So...what happened?" he asked, careful not to look at her.

"I found the girl. She was in a cottage with some guy the family knew. He'd abducted her on her way home from school...didn't Matt tell you all this?" She frowned at him.

Mitch nodded and sat down opposite her. "Yeah, he covered all that. I'm wondering what happened to you?"

Shannon shook her head. "I wish I knew. It's always been so easy before and this time it was...I can't describe it. I felt like it was draining me." She chewed on her lip and sipped her coffee, watching him under lashes. "Maybe I'm losing my gift."

Mitch scowled at the table. "You were probably just tired, Shan. And having Matt Carter watching your every move probably didn't help."

"You don't trust him?" asked Shannon, her eyes wide.

Mitch shook his head. "I don't know what his agenda is, why Lewis sent him, and that bugs me. He also seems to have an unhealthy interest in you and your ability."

"He did ask a lot of questions about it," Shannon admitted.

"You see?" Mitch stood up from the table and strode to the window, resting on his knuckles as he looked out over the back yard. "Don't trust him, Shannon. I know he looks like butter wouldn't melt but I don't think he's here by accident."

Shannon frowned. "But he did seem genuinely concerned about me," she said softly.

Mitch turned back from the window. "Well, of course he did. You know how this goes, Shannon. You're property that they want back and maybe his brief is to infiltrate us, gain your trust and lure you away back to Lewis Carter. Or perhaps he's on a rec – sussing out the set up and keeping an eye on you 'till they can come and get you."

Shannon looked up at him. "You think he's capable of that?"

"Like father like son, Shan."

Shannon dropped her head and Mitch studied her for a moment, puzzled. Then the penny dropped. "You think he actually likes you?" he asked.

She shrugged.

Mitch laughed. "Oh, c'mon Shan. You're not some little naïve kid anymore. He's not your knight in shining armour come to whisk you off to some golden future where you're a normal woman with a husband, kids, a yard to brush and dogs to walk."

Shannon stood up quickly. "Well, if I am losing this curse then why couldn't I find someone like Matt and be normal?"

Mitch frowned at her. He came around the table and pulled her into his embrace, folding her head against his heart. "Hush, Shannon. I didn't mean to upset you." He pulled her up to look at him, his hands on either side of her face. "I don't think you're losing your ability, sweetheart and even if you are…you know I'd look after you. You could have a normal life with me."

Shannon sighed and slid away from him. "But Mitch," she said softly. "You've never considered me to be normal."

Mitch watched her leave the kitchen, keeping a tight rein on his temper for as long as he could and then he lunged at the table, swiping her cup off it and sending it flying across the kitchen until it finally smashed on the tiled floor. He stood for a moment, leaning on the table until his breathing had calmed and then he reached into his pocket for his phone and called Grace.

****

Sean waited in the car as his mother and father talked inside the caravan. They were at Camac Valley and the caravan belonged to a friend of Grace's. It was a good place to meet but having his parents together was making Sean strangely uneasy. He knew that it was necessary if they were all going to get what they needed – years of careful planning had brought them this far, Shannon was within their reach. All that they needed now was to get the go ahead from the rest of the leadership and then the final phase of the plan could get underway – Shannon Reeves would disappear never to be seen again and their movement would be unstoppable.

The door of the caravan opened and Mitch came out and walked towards the car. His head was down and his shoulders were hunched. Sean didn't know if that was a bad sign or not – his father was hard to read.

Grace pulled the door closed, nodding to her son as she did so and Sean started the engine, pulling smoothly away once Mitch had closed his door and fastened his seatbelt.

They drove in silence for a few miles.

"So, what's the story?" asked Sean finally. "Are we on or what?"

Mitch sighed. "They've agreed to a meet."

Sean raised his eyebrows. "That was fast. It seems positive then?"

Mitch made a face. "I dunno, Sean. You know what it's like. Get them on a bad day and you're likely to get your head blown off."

Sean sighed. "So where and when?"

"This coming Friday in some club called the 'Warehouse'. You know it?"

Sean nodded. "Aye, fancy place that. Busy too. Is mam sure that she can…"

Mitch rolled his eyes at Sean. "You really think I questioned your mother's judgment about where to meet?" He shook his head. "I'm on her mercy, remember? If this goes well then we're sorted and I can come home. If not then we're all screwed."

Sean nodded. "So what's the plan for this week?"

Mitch sighed. "You'd better tell Erin to get some glad rags organised. She might need to take Shannon shopping. We're all going on a night out."

****

Sean's announcement was greeted at first by silence and then Erin whooped with excitement. "The Warehouse? On Friday? New clothes? Yes!" She punched the air and Matt laughed.

Erin's delight was contagious and soon she and Shannon were talking shoes and jewellery and what colours were 'in' and what shapes would suit their very different figures.

Mitch pulled out a wallet and handed Shannon a credit card. "Knock yourself out, Princess. It's been a long time since we had a night out."

Shannon's smile faded and she looked at him incredulously. She looked around the others, her face flushing, and then set the credit card on the table, turned on her heel and walked out and into the back garden.

Mitch frowned. "What did I say?" he asked in astonishment.

Sean and Matt found other things to look at in the kitchen but Erin was shaking her head at Mitch. "You don't know?" He shook his head. "You bloody men are all the same – clueless! Even if you are bankrolling her clothes and stuff, you didn't have to make it so obvious in front of us. You treated her like she was about sixteen and you were her dad." Still shaking her head, Erin went upstairs to raid her wardrobe.

Mitch looked at Sean and Matt. "You think maybe I should apologise?"

Sean shook his head. "Nah, leave it. She'll calm down and you two'll be bosom buddies again in no time. You go out there now and you'll just stir it all up again, make it worse."

Mitch sighed and rubbed his eyes. "When did you get so wise, Sean?" He punched his son playfully on the arm and Sean grinned.

Matt stood up silently, poured two mugs of strong coffee and headed outside with them. Mitch watched him go, a frown settling on his brow.

"Let it go, Dad," Sean told him softly.

Mitch shrugged. "What if I don't want to? What if I think it's dangerous?"

Sean looked up at him. "I don't get you."

"It's not just jealousy, Sean. Yeah, okay, I still …have feelings for her but there's another reason I don't like whatever it is that's developing between them." Mitch sat down heavily. "I don't trust Lewis Carter. That man does nothing without good reason so him sending Matt wasn't just a spur-of-the-moment decision. There's something behind it."

"You think Matt's a spy here?" Sean sat up a little straighter.

Mitch shifted in his chair. "I dunno. I can't figure him out. Either he's clueless about Lewis's plans and he does fancy her, or he's got a mission here and Shannon's part of it, in which case he's a better bloody actor than I ever gave him credit for."

"You used to trust him," Sean said sullenly.

Mitch nodded. "Yeah, I did. He was a good soldier but we're on different sides now and I'm not sure if he realises that or not."

"If he does?"

"Then we got trouble."

****

Shannon was sitting on an ancient swing seat, a grey cardigan wrapped around her. Matt handed her a coffee and sat down beside her without a word.

"What's on your mind?" He asked finally.

Shannon gave a tight half-smile. "I'm running out of time," she said softly.

Matt frowned. "To do what?"

She sighed and sat right back, the swing tipped a little and then settled into a soothing rhythm. Matt shifted back beside her. "I'm going to trust you, Matt. I wasn't sure that I could before but it seems like you said nothing to Mitch about our little conversation the other night so I'm going to have to take that as proof that you'll help and not turn me over to them once you find out what the plan is."

"The plan? There's a plan?"

"Well, when I say 'plan' I mean that most of this is guess work by me. I managed to get in touch with Denton while I was on assignment about eight months ago. I told him what I thought was going on and he told me to stick with it until he could find verifiable proof, make some calls, and pull in some folks he could trust. You know how it is. He also told me to expect some heat 'cause once word got around there would obviously be someone somewhere who would take the decision to come get me before I could be brainwashed by Mitch's people and do any damage."

"So that's what I was sent to warn you about?"

"Exactly. Mitch has always been waiting for something like this to happen anyway – ever since he pulled all the contacts – so he took it all in his stride and I figured that, if they sent you, it was a message to me that they had what they needed and they were ready to make their move on Mitch's organisation. Although, I suppose we should really call it Grace's organisation 'cause she seems to be calling most of the shots."

Matt raised an eyebrow. "Really? I thought it was Sean."

Shannon shook her head. "He's high up obviously and there are probably wallets that Grace has to answer to but in general she's the boss."

"And you think I was sent to let you know that they were ready?"

"Maybe. That's what I thought at the time anyway. Maybe because you and Mitch had a connection too."

Matt nodded. "Our past guaranteed me safe passage."

"And you came to him via Sean – that was genius."

"No, that was necessity. I didn't have any other contacts here."

"Whatever. He trusts you. To a point."

"Yeah," Matt grinned. "I wouldn't push that whole trust thing too much. Very little would send him the other way."

Shannon bit her lip. "Yeah, that might be dangerous."

Matt turned to face her. "So the plan involves me getting on Mitch's wrong side?"

Shannon nodded. "Well, it didn't until they announced the whole night out thing."

"Care to explain. I feel like you're talking riddles."

"Sorry." She took a deep breath and chewed on her lip a little more. Matt found himself staring and forced himself to turn away slightly. "I don't think will just be an innocent night out, I think it's a meet – the organisation wanting to check out the prodigal son, figure out if his claims are true and whether or not it's enough to get him accepted back into the fold. They got their proof, more or less, when I found Shauna so now they're going to meet Mitch."

"In a nightclub?" Matt wasn't convinced.

"Depends on the club. You know they have their fingers in a lot of pies and this place could be one of them. If so then it's a deceptively controllable meeting place. They could fill it with their own people and it would just look like any other club."

He nodded slowly. "Okay, I can see that. So what's the problem?"

"If Mitch stays calm, manages to convince them that he can bring them a glorious future, that he's worth another chance just from bringing me to them, then it could all be decided on Friday night. I could be chained up and stuck in some Dublin basement by Saturday morning. You'd be dumped in an alley somewhere with a bullet in your skull and none of their enemies would be safe again."

"Jesus."

"Yeah."

"You could refuse to do what they want."

Shannon looked at him sadly. "I don't have to be conscious to do it, Matt. They could hook me up to a machine that knocks me out but keeps me alive, slip your president's toothbrush into my hand and I wouldn't be able to stop myself. Mitch knows how it works for me – once I'm there, in that person's world, I just start talking." She sighed.

"But Mitch doesn't know that you can…" Matt began.

"No!" Shannon glanced towards the house in alarm. "He doesn't know the half of what I'm capable of."

Matt thought about that for a moment. He drank his now-cold coffee and stared out across the garden. How had he managed to get in the middle of this again? Ah, yes, dear old Dad. He'd have to buy him a new tie to thank him. Shaking his head, Matt turned back to Shannon. She was watching him intently, her eyes troubled and her hands twisting around each other in agitation. Matt reached out and set his hand on top of hers. "So what's your incredibly dangerous plan then?" he asked and was startled to see her blush.

Moving her hands from under his, Shannon wriggled forwards on the seat, moving the swing a little faster for a moment. "Well, I was thinking that the best thing to do is kind of throw him a little curve ball. Knock him off his game a little. If he doesn't make a good impression on Friday night then it'll take longer for all this to get sorted out. I could get in touch with Denton in the meantime and try to…impress on him the need to make a move sooner rather than later."

Matt nodded. "Logical plan. So how're we going to knock Mitch off a little? Where do I come into all this?"

She was chewing on her lip again. "Well, you saw how he's been recently. He doesn't usually act so possessive but since you came along he seems to be a little …um…" she spread her hands and let out a long breath.

Matt cocked his head and looked at her, a slow smile spreading across his face. "You think he's jealous? Of me?" Matt laughed.

Shannon rubbed her face with her hands. "I'm glad you think it's funny."

Matt calmed a little but he couldn't quite stop himself from grinning happily at her. "Sorry, it's just that Mitch Cooper having a crisis of confidence because of me strikes me as hilarious."

Shannon sighed. "What he did in there with the credit card? That's not him. And the pda's when we were in Donegal? I don't even know if he realises that he's doing it."

Matt screwed his face up. "Rewind there a minute. Pda's?"

Shannon nodded. "Public displays of affection. Don't you text?"

"Not about pda's."

Shannon grinned. "So, what I was thinking is that if we turn the heat up a little then it might piss him off enough to have him on his toes on Friday night. The more interested he is in what's happening with us, the less likely he is to be able to push things forward with Grace and her gang."

"So you want us to flirt a little, dance to a few slow songs?" he leaned a little closer to her, grinning. Shannon smiled in spite of herself.

"I know it'll be difficult for you but yeah, if you tried to show a little bit of interest and I pretended to find you attractive…"

"Pretended?" Matt put a hand to his heart. "God, woman you've mortally wounded me."

Shannon giggled. "Oh, you'll recover, Romeo." She became serious again. "The thing is…well, I kindda laid the groundwork a little, tested the waters so to speak."

"And?"

"And I think it might work."

"And that's a good thing, right?" Matt frowned. "Although I'm hearing in your voice that it's not a good thing."

"Well, I also made it out that I might be losing my gift and that I wasn't exactly sad about it 'cause maybe without it I could, y'know, get married, have kids and a normal life. With you." She looked up at him shyly and grinned nervously. "It had the desired effect – got him thinking and hopefully worrying, but I'm worried that it might all backfire."

"In what way?"

"Well, he's not known for his agreeable personality."

Matt laughed softly. "No, that's true. Mitch was always the shoot first and ask questions later type. Wait a minute," he looked up at her. "You think he'd shoot me?!"

"Um, no. Well, yes. I mean, maybe. I don't know how he'd deal with seeing us…together. I mean, he's under pressure as it is – he needs to deliver and he's waited a long time to do it. On the outside he's pretty calm but I reckon that inside he's stressing a lot more than he likes to let on."

"So maybe tipping things too far would send him for the nearest holster?"

"Maybe."

"And you think that I couldn't handle myself if things got rough?"

She had the good grace to flush. "Well, it's been a long time since you were in that kind of situation and I …"

"Want to send me back to daddy in one piece?"

Shannon's eyes narrowed. "Unlike your dad, I don't use people as pawns, Matt."

"So why am I here?"

"Because I didn't know what else to do. I didn't know if you were part of the grand scheme or not." She sat back in the seat and folded her arms, looking away from him.

Matt sighed. He felt guilty as hell for flaring up like a six year old but part of his anger was directed at himself – maybe she was right, he was out of shape. "I'm sorry," he told her. "I shouldn't have jumped down your throat like that."

Shannon shook her head. "It's okay. I'm not what you could call gifted at human interaction."

They grinned at each other. "So, are we gonna do this?" Matt asked.

Shannon nodded. "So long as you think it's a good idea."

"Best one we've got. Think you can get word to Dent?"

She nodded. "I'm going to get Erin to take me shopping – I'll make sure I get a chance then."

"Think you'll be allowed?" Matt swallowed a smirk.

"I think they'll put me on a tight leash and Erin'll be told to keep a close eye but yeah, I'll be allowed. Mitch will want to keep on my good side." She stood up and lifted the coffee mugs. "We should get inside. We've already got their attention."

Matt nodded and followed her in. At the door he leaned over and whispered "Do we get to kiss on Friday night?"

Shannon grinned at his flirtatious tone. "Only if you shave, get a haircut, make an effort…"

Matt's breath tickled her neck. "Tease," he whispered.

Chapter Sixteen

Lewis Carter stood in the VIP lounge of the International Airport looking through the smoked glass at the tide of humanity passing through on their way to baggage collection.

Although grey haired and feeling the odd twinge of arthritis around his knuckles and hips, he was no less impressive a figure than he had been when he had first taken the helm of special ops some thirty years earlier. He stood with his legs slightly apart, arms folded, head slightly lowered and back straight. He looked like a bull about to charge.

"Mr Carter?" The young woman barely reached his shoulder. She was pretty in an immaculate-over-made-up way. He smiled at her and nodded, wondering what Marilyn would've made of the way this young woman, more than half his age, was looking up at him through her long lashes.

"Your car is out front for you, Sir," she said, her cheeks dimpling as she smiled back at him.

Lewis stood for a second more, savouring the calm and quiet of the lounge and then she was opening the door and the noise and smell of several thousand tired and impatient travellers hit him.

They walked to the exit without speaking, his escort falling in around him unobtrusively. All three were wearing shades. Outside, Frank was standing by the rear door of a nondescript blue Vectra. He was wearing shades too. Lewis nodded to him and got a brief dip of his head in return. A further two plain hire cars were parked behind the Vectra, both were filled with his men, making up an unofficial unit.

These were good men, men he trusted, and they were here at his request with no idea what was going down. Lewis sighed and turned to the young woman at his side. Her eyes widened slightly as she watched the three tall men in sunglasses file around her and climb into the Vectra and its twin parked in front.

"Tanya," Lewis said and the young woman snapped back to attention. "Thank you for your courtesy today. I've been very impressed with the way our little visit has been handled. You're a credit to the airport, young lady, and I'll be sure to let your superiors know."

Tanya blushed and her dimples flashed again. She looked up at him and licked her lips delicately. "It's been our pleasure, Sir. I hope we see you again," she said breathily, her eyes locking with his.

Lewis took her hand and pressed his lips to the back of it very gently. "I hope so too," he said, then released her hand and folded his six feet two inch frame into the back seat in an easy fluid movement.

The car swept away from the pavement leaving Tanya gaping behind them, her hand still hanging in mid-air.

Lewis opened the small valise at his feet and began to shuffle the papers inside. He glanced up at the back of Frank's head.

"How long have we known each other, Frank?" he asked.

"Fifteen years, Sir," came the curt reply.

"A lesser man would've sniggered, maybe even shook his head at my little display back there," observed Lewis, pulling on a pair of reading glasses.

"I'm not a lesser man, Sir," replied Frank moving out of the traffic and accelerating into the countryside.

"And Marilyn?" mused Lewis. "If she'd been here to see me kiss a young lady's hand? What would she have said, do you think?" Lewis paused in his perusal of the report in his hand and glanced up at his two front seat companions.

"She would've rolled her eyes, called you and old flirt and asked when we could stop for a coffee," said Frank smoothly, his expression never changing.

Lewis nodded. "Yes, she would. She's a good woman, my wife. And a smart one. Now, get Denton on the phone and let's get to… where are we going?"

"Ballykelly, Sir. Line's ringing." Frank listened until the phone connected and then switched off his ear piece. In the passenger seat his colleague closed his eyes behind his shades and caught a five minute nap.

****

Lewis Carter entered the large room on Ballykelly Army Base at a trot. Eight men crowded in behind him carrying various items of equipment. Lewis stood in the middle of the room, issuing pistol-quick commands as the men took off around the room and the techs already in position turned in their seats or stood to watch. Carter looked like the centre of a whirlwind, the eye of a storm.

Denton Fraser sat back in his chair by the window, laced his fingers behind his head and watched the show, smiling. Like Carter he had worn a suit and tie – no matter what his kids said, people took you seriously when the threads were good. Unlike Carter, Fraser had discarded both the suit jacket and his tie about an hour earlier. His pristine white shirtsleeves were rolled up, there was a pen behind his ear and the desk in front of him was spread with an overlapping array of maps, reports and surveillance photographs.

Carter was finally silent. He stood with his arms folded, watching with interest until the last piece of equipment was installed and the young soldiers had left the room. Finally he turned his attention to the others in the room, his gaze landing on Fraser.

"What?" asked Carter, trying not to grin.

"You're damned impressive, man," said Fraser. "I can see why they like you so much up on Capitol Hill."

Carter unfolded his arms and slid into the chair opposite his friend. "You know where my heart is, Dent."

Fraser nodded. "From the moment you first called me about this, and that was a long time ago, I knew we'd end up in a room like this, surrounded by paper in a town with a name that I can say but probably can't spell. I also knew that it would be a black op and before you start on your guilt trip, the rest of these guys knew it too." He grinned at Lewis. "We have some good men with us, Lew. We just need a plan."

Lewis chewed on a fingernail and nodded. "Ok." He took a deep breath, exhaled and then stood up. "Right, what have we got?

I wanna hear it from the beginning in as much detail as you can manage."

Fraser stood up, all business now. He signalled to two of the techs on the other side of the room and directed Lewis Carter's focus to the four large screens at the back of the room. A map appeared on the first screen – a satellite image of the earth. The image sharpened to detail of Europe, then cycled into an image of Ireland, Dublin and then a Dublin street.

"Timeline," Fraser began and a bullet-point list appeared on the next screen. Fraser pointed to the map screen and then to the first point. "Fouteen o four local time last Monday I took a call. It came from a coffee shop on Grafton Street in Dublin. The phone that was used is unregistered. Caller was Rebecca Morgan."

"I think we should keep that name out of it for now," Lewis was frowning.

Fraser nodded, a keyboard clicked and on-screen the name was changed to Shannon Reeves.

Carter nodded. "Ok. Carry on."

"Caller asked if I was recording. I wasn't. Caller then requested that I record the conversation as she had a message for Lewis Carter. Fraser glanced briefly in Carter's direction and nodded to someone on the far side of the room. The third screen lit up. Shannon's voice rang out around the room, distorted slightly by the cubicle that she had hidden in. In the background Carter could hear the muffled thump, thump, thump of a traditional musical beat. On the screen each sound was characterised by a spike on the voice modulation program.

"Designation Stargate, authorisation 4479865240." Shannon was saying, her voice was breathy, each syllable rushed.

"She didn't have much time," said Carter softly.

There was a pause, a door squeaked open and shut again, water ran. There was nothing but the whistle of static for almost twenty seconds and then Shannon spoke again, her voice a low whisper. "Lewis, when you get this, it's time to move. I don't know if I was supposed to keep Matt with me or not but I did and, well, Mitch's become a bit...territorial. We're going to use that to force him to make a move and show his hand so I think you'll need to be ready soon. We'll all be at the Warehouse club this Friday night but for God's sake don't have your guys anywhere near it. If you do it'll end up being a blood bath. Mitch wouldn't organise a night out for no reason so I'm guessing it's a meet for the organisation. Don't make your move until we have all the players but you should be able to get some good surveillance. Just stay back, please. Oh, I should tell you the address we're staying at. God, how could I forget that? I'm losing my mind." She laughed, a tight, hard sound that made Carter grimace. "Farnham Walk, number 4. I need to go soon, Erin's waiting for me." Denton's voice cut in on the line, "Who's Erin?"

"What? Oh, um, Erin Heaney. Brendan Heaney's granddaughter." She sighed. "I've been going over and over it in my head and I just can't see why they would delay for much longer anyway. The back-up team's gone so as far as they know it's just me."

Fraser spoke to her again. "Do you think you're in danger? Shouldn't we just come get you out of there?"

"Oh, no, no, no, no. I think we're safe so long as they think I'm isolated. I want to play this our way. We need to be able to control things more than we're doing. You could still take some of them down with the Intel we've already got but we couldn't be sure to get them all. I'm just worried that it's not going to be safe for much longer."

"We can get you both on Friday, Shannon," Fraser's voice was louder, tight with anxiety.

'And what about taking them out? This is our opportunity, Dent."

Fraser's sigh echoed in the room. "Look, I'll check into it. We'll base up north somewhere. It'll be a, well, a small group."

"In the black?"

"I would imagine so. Listen, I've been checking into the group and there's some stuff you need to know…"

"Shannon? Are you in here?" It was a woman's voice. Carter's head went up.

"Yeah, yeah, just give me a second," Shannon shouted and then whispered into the phone. "Remember what I said. Stay out of it for now. If anything goes wrong then Matt and I will get to the North Star Hotel on Amiens Street and you can pick us up there. Otherwise, stay out of it and hopefully we can get them all, Dent. Tell Lewis Carter that I want to negotiate…

"Shannon!" the woman's voice again, louder this time.

The connection was broken and the lines on the screen dissolved.

Carter stood still for a moment, his face was dark. He cleared his throat before he spoke. "Get the others in here. Three teams to cover the house, the club and all the routes north. We need to be ready to go and take these bastards out."

Chapter Seventeen

Shannon had been standing in the shower for almost twenty minutes. The water was hot, cascading over her body and easing some of the stress. She wondered where Matt was.

They'd been keeping a low profile for the past few days – doing little more than eating at the same table. On occasion she'd looked up to find his eyes on her but he'd looked away quickly when he knew she'd caught him. Mitch had been glued to her side since Sunday night, dropping little kisses onto her cheeks and little caresses along her arms. It made her shiver thinking about it.

She'd actually enjoyed the little shopping expedition with Erin on Monday – it had been short (just over an hour) but Erin had been lively company and the shops had been wonderful. Thankfully they'd stopped for a coffee in Bewley's and she'd managed to phone Denton from the ladies, throwing the phone away straight afterwards. They'd returned home exuberant about their purchases with Erin chattering nineteen to the dozen about how gorgeous she was going to look on Friday and how Sean would 'take a second notion of her'. Mitch had laughed and investigated the contents of their bags.

Sean had been slightly more reserved, watching the goings on from behind his newspaper, his sullen eyes following Shannon around the living room as she slipped from Mitch's clutches and escaped to her room before he could find the outfit she'd chosen. Matt had been loitering in the doorway of the kitchen, an ever-present mug of coffee in his hand. She had given him a brief nod to let him know that she'd managed to make the call and then headed for the stairs.

And now it was Friday, the men had headed out to find clothes for tonight and hopefully a barber for Matt. She grinned. As they'd left, Matt had made a point of asking Shannon if she thought he might be allowed a dance later. The heat in his eyes had momentarily made her catch her breath before she reminded herself that it was all just an act. Mitch had already been out in the car but Sean had heard the question and her reply and had, no doubt, reported it all back to Mitch. At least she hoped he had.

She exhaled and leaned her forehead against the cool tiles, letting the strong jets of water flow over her tense shoulders and back. She was trying not to think about later too much, there was a chance that she would lose her nerve. There were a lot of things to be afraid of – messing things up could end up with Matt dead, not messing things up could end up with Matt dead. And either way she could end up chained to a wall somewhere. Shannon pounded a tile with her fist. The idea of being at the mercy of these people forever made her feel ill. To hell with bringing them down; she should've run away, just left when she'd had the chance, jumped on a plane, bullied Lewis Carter into hiding her or finding her a new identity again - but then she would never have been truly safe. She would never have been able to relax because she knew that Mitch wouldn't just let her go. He would've followed her and, someday, he would've found her again.

Shannon drew in a shuddering breath and reached for the shampoo again. She needed to calm down or she was going to really screw things up. Turning her face into the steady stream of water she lathered her hair again, her fingers working across her head and then down through the strands. She rinsed the suds out and twisted her hair around her hand to get rid of some of the water. One more thorough wash with the chocolate scented shower gel that she'd picked up on Monday and she'd be done. Now, where'd she put it?

As she turned around, Shannon heard a noise – just audible above the pounding of the shower. Frowning she spotted the gel and lifted the tube, listening intently.

There it was again – a click, almost like the sound of a door being carefully closed. Mitch? Squinting through the curtain and the steamy room, Shannon squeezed some gel onto her hand. If it was Mitch and he made a move to come in here she was going to slap some of this into his eyes – pity to waste good shower gel but, hey, needs must.

"Shannon?" Matt's voice was soft but sounded surprisingly close. She jumped and then breathed a sigh of relief.

"Jeez, Matt. You trying to give me a heart attack. I thought you were Mitch."

She thought she heard him chuckle. "Relax, it's only me. I thought that, since I'm going to seduce you later, I should drop by and get an advance screening, y'know. Make sure all the hassle's going to be worth it."

"Ho, ho, ho. Very witty. You almost got a face full of chocolate scented shower gel."

"Chocolate scented, eh? So you're going to smell good enough to eat later."

"Are you going to quit flirting long enough for me to tell you what I've arranged with Denton?" Shannon was smiling; Matt could hear it in her voice.

"Oh, okay then. I was just getting in some practice – it's been a while."

"Really? I would never have been able to tell."

"There you go again, Shannon, breaking my heart with your harsh words."

"Matt…"

"Yes, sorry. I'm listening."

"I told them what was going down and what I'm afraid of. I've suggested that, if it doesn't go according to plan, we'll meet them in the bar of the North Star Hotel on Amiens Street."

"They have a team here?"

"Close by but they'll stay back on Friday night. I don't want a lot of shooting to start in case there are civilians in the club. I mean, we don't know what the set up is going to be and how Mitch will really react. Maybe this is a bad idea; do you think this is a bad idea? 'Cause if you do then we should just call it all off. You know where Amiens Street is don't you? If something goes wrong then you get yourself out and away, ok?" There was silence. Shannon wondered if he was still there. "You still awake out there or am I boring you?"

"You're afraid," he said finally.

Shannon sighed. "Yes, a little. I don't want anyone to die because of me but I don't want to be left with Mitch's people either."

"Then we take the chance tonight, Shannon. It's a good plan and I think it'll work. Yes, Mitch is unpredictable but we can handle him. Okay?"

Shannon nodded and put the cap back on the shower gel. She'd been in the shower so long that she was starting to wrinkle. "What time is it, Matt?"

He checked his watch. "Just after four. What time are we heading out?"

"Pass me the towel, will you? Thanks. Erin suggested a meal around eight, a few drinks and then on to the club around ten thirty or eleven."

Matt clapped his hands. "Right. Best let you get on then. Obviously you're going to need a bit of work on the face and stuff if you want me to seduce you."

Shannon folded the towel around herself and grinned. "Oh, you poor boy. You really don't know what you're in for do you. When you see me walk down those stairs tonight, you're going to have major problems lifting your tongue off the floor."

Matt's low laugh sent a tingle down her spine. "There you go again, Shannon. You can talk the talk but I think you're just a little tease who won't deliver some action when the time comes." He ignored her grunt of disgust. "Truthfully I'm beginning to wonder if I might not be a bit too much of a challenge for you. After all, it has been quite a while since you got to party with a real man."

Shannon couldn't stop the giggle that escaped the hand she had pressed to her mouth. She was about to respond but two soft clicks told her that Matt had left. She turned the shower off feeling a lot more light hearted than she had been ten minutes earlier. It was almost time to get ready.

****

Three miles away, in the attic of a home belonging to a sympathiser, Grace Connor took off a set of headphones and smiled to herself. Her idea to bug the house in Farnham Walk without anyone-else knowing about it had just paid off.

"Gotcha," she whispered.

"Do we tell the boss? Or yer man Connor?" asked the young man beside her, lifting one side of his own head set.

Grace tapped her teeth with a well-manicured nail. She finally shook her head. "No, we'll just be ready." She flipped open her phone and speed dialled. It rang once before it was picked up. "Blade? Change of plan. We're taking the girl tonight." She closed the phone, her mind whirring ahead.

Turning back to the surveillance system that they'd set up she nodded for the tech-head to go back to work. As soon as he turned away, Grace pulled a silenced weapon from her Jackie O inspired coat and shot him twice in the head, careful to stay away from the blood splatter. He was no longer useful and he'd already heard too much. She flipped the phone open again. "Tony? Clean up at Pat Donaghy's place. Attic room. There's equipment to be destroyed too. No, Tony later isn't good enough. Get your arse round here now."

She snapped the phone shut and left the room, closing the door behind her. By the time she'd left the house through the back door, the dead man was forgotten and she was planning what to wear to the club. Tonight was going to be fun.

Chapter Eighteen

Lewis Carter was talking on the phone. Correction: Lewis Carter was bellowing on the phone. His face was puce, his eyes wild. All around the room heads were bowed low over keyboards, staying out of the line of fire.

Denton Fraser was no exception. He had been staring at the same inch on the Dublin map for almost ten minutes. Carter had started yelling about eight minutes ago. Fraser figured that whoever had found himself on the receiving end of Carter's call was either a major player, stubborn or had a death wish."Have you been listening to a word I've said?" asked Carter at top volume. He had long since discarded the jacket of his expensive suit, along with his tie, cufflinks and, most recently, two buttons on his shirt. Fraser cringed. He knew this scene. The guy on the other end of the phone had managed to push every one of Lewis Carter's buttons. Carter had reached his limit. The hammer was about to fall.

"I see," Carter hissed. He paused, calmed himself with a visible effort and then began speaking slowly and precisely into the phone. "How about I patch a call through to our Commander in Chief and let him know just how many assholes in his security services are willing to put his life at risk, and the lives of his family and just about every other major fucking world leader he cares to mention? How about that, Howard?" Carter spat out the name and then listened for a moment. "Uh-huh. What a fucking fabulous idea, pal. You do that. I'll be waiting for his call." Carter shook his head and waved a finger in the air, as though 'Howard' was standing in front of him. "No, no, again you're not listening you slimy little weasel. I don't want to speak to you any more you snivelling little coward. I want to speak to your superior. If I ever have to listen to your whining again, I will personally see to it that your skinny little ass is bounced out of your shithole of an office faster than you ever thought possible. Did you hear THAT, Howard? Yeah, I fucking bet you did." Carter closed his phone with a snap and flung it onto the desk. He stood for a few seconds, breathing loudly, hands on his hips. He studied his shoes and took several deep breaths. Sensing the silence in the room, he looked around. "And that, ladies and gentlemen, is the main problem that I have with mobile phones."

"What's that Sir?" asked Fraser.

Lewis reached out and picked up his phone, jiggling it around in his hand. "Snapping this little thing closed just doesn't do it for me. I need a good solid receiver to slam down." he said.

Around the room there were grins and nods of agreement, shoulders relaxed and fingers began to type again. Carter sat down facing the 'story board' as he called it. Where Fraser was content to use all the tech and the big screens, Carter still preferred an old school approach to remind him where he was. As a result they had pulled chairs and tables away from a corner of the room and put up a large cork board courtesy of the army base. It was now almost completely covered with information – photographs of Mitch, Sean, Matt, Shannon, Grace, anyone and everyone connected with the house at Farnham Walk or the splinter group that Sean Connor apparently ran. On top of each photo was a post-it detailing the latest sighting of the individual. There was a street map of Dublin with almost forty map tacks on it now – houses belonging to each member of the splinter group, any shop, restaurant or newsagent's that any of them had been sighted in and other places of interest. On the left was a batch of satellite surveillance photos of Sean Connor's house, Grace's house, Shannon's in Portstewart, the Warehouse Club. Anything they could use. Anything with a connection. It was an organised jumble of images and information. Looking at it helped Carter to think. Looking at it gave Fraser a headache.

Carter walked over to the story board and let his eyes go over everything again. He lingered briefly on the crystal clear 7" by 5" enlargement of Shannon and Erin in Bewley's. Shannon looked relaxed, another shopper out enjoying tracking down a few bargains. Until you looked at her eyes; a world of worry shone out of them and Lewis bit his lower lip – if he could tell just by looking at a photo then surely Mitch Cooper could too. He turned back to the room.

The computers were busy. Decoding taped phone calls and clandestine recordings, touching base with informers, contacts, people you could lean on. Frank was at the third station from the door. As Lewis watched he leaned back, took off his omnipresent shades and rubbed his eyes. He looked in Carter's direction.

"Got somethin' Frank?" Carter strode over and looked over his shoulder. Frank was on the web, in a chat room link charmingly named "Terror Is Us".

"World's a fucked up place, Sir," Frank said.

Carter grinned. "You won't get any argument from me on that one."

Frank tapped the screen with his pen. "You ever heard of this dude? Someone they call 'Blade'?"

Carter turned sharply towards Fraser who had stood up.

"Haven't heard that name in a while." Fraser moved closer.

"Yeah, well this is the third time I've come across it." Frank was watching the screen as more cyber-chat rolled up.

"In what context?" Carter's mind was racing.

"Um, this place is like a grapevine, a rumour mill for terrorists." Frank looked up at Carter. "They may be crazy, sadistic fuckers but they still have the urge to gossip." Carter raised an eyebrow.

"Cute," said Fraser. "What's the rumour?"

Frank scrolled back through several conversations and brought up some highlighted text. "Ok, it's obviously all in code but the gist is that some dude called 'Rogue' is keen to break bread with 'Tuesday's Child' and your guy 'Blade' has sent my guy here a message saying, er, "Ard choille" whatever that means, um…" Frank scrolled through more text, "Yeah, this was weird. There's some 'en prise' involved but apparently it's all 'zugzwang' right now so there's no point in pushing forward unless anyone has any kind of plan to remove the 'pin'." Frank made a face.

Fraser shook his head. "Anything else?"

"Gibberish, geek speak. I thought I had a location reference, like map co-ordinates."

"And?"

Frank grinned sheepishly. "It's a jumbled up phone number. At least that's what I'm thinking now. Right number of digits, I just can't work them all out. Tom has his number cruncher doin' the business but it'll take a while."

Carter began pacing, everyone stilled and the tension in the room rose a notch. After hours of waiting, his men felt the change in the air. The boss was about to issue orders. They leaned forward in their seats.

"Okay," Carter began, "These geeks you've been monitoring, can we trace any of them to a home address?"

Frank looked across the room. "Nick?"

A small, weedy man wearing glasses and a seventies tie smiled over the top of his monitor. "On it, Sir."

"Right," Carter continued, "I want as much Intel on these guys as you can dig up and I need it yesterday. Get names, check with NCIC so we know who we're dealing with. It's a complex search protocol so get Harvey to help you if you need it." Nick nodded and bent to his keyboard. Carter gestured to one of the other techs, "Work with him, get onto a DMV database – we need a current photo and address. Use Net-Intel, I wanna know every site these guys have even touched on the last twelve months. We need background, we need a way in and these guys know what's going on inside this organisation so we need them. Got that?"

There was a collective shout of "Sir," from around the room.

"Fraser we need a pick up location and three or four routes out."

Fraser nodded and returned to his monitor. "On it, Sir."

"Joel, this code that the geeks were writing in. Get onto that. I wanna know who the Pin is, who Tuesday's Child is. Follow the code. Frank, stay with these guys, follow them around and..."

"Sir," Frank said loudly and the room stilled again. "I want to be clear. Are you authorising a tracer?"

Carter eyeballed him for a few seconds and then grinned. "Whatever it takes, ladies and gentlemen. Make contact in four hours. I want results then." He checked his watch. "We'll have to go with whatever we have 3 hours after that. I'm contacting Shannon or Matt at midnight so we damn well better have a plan by then. Everyone-else?" he gestured around the room at the expectant faces. "If you have tech then we need travel to Dublin, transport to and from the pick-up. At least two changes and decoys. Travel from Belfast to LAX night after next for 3. Three more each subsequent night 'till we're all home. Transport from LAX to a safe house for the principals. If you don't have tech then get your gear together ready for a move when I give the order. I'm sure I don't need to tell you that this could be messy but…" his phone began to ring. Frowning, Carter picked it off the table and flipped it open. "What?" He smiled and stood a little straighter, head high. "It's good of you to call, Sir. Yes, we do need some clearance and perhaps some diplomatic intercession and, yes sir, I understand." A pause, Carter listened, head to the side, expression neutral and eyes narrowed. "Yes, Sir, I'm aware of that but I think it only fair to be honest and tell you that if I don't get the help I'll just go on ahead and do it my own way." He listened again. "Frankly, Sir, I don't care. I believed the Intel and I got my son involved because no-one else would cut through the red tape in time. I'm through waitin' Sir. No, I don't believe I'm being disrespectful at all but Sir, Sir? Sir?" Carter took the phone from his ear and rolled his eyes.

Fraser saw the colour spread up his neck and over his face. Grimacing, he crouched over his keyboard and waited for the explosion.

Carter put the phone back to his ear. "Do I get the clearance?" he asked evenly. He sighed. "Cut the crap, Sir. Do I get the damn clearance or not?" Grinning, Carter gave the room a thumbs up. "Yes, Sir. Thank you, Sir. It's been a pleasure talkin' to you." He closed his phone and walked back to his storyboard. Time to come up with a plan.

Chapter Nineteen

Erin knocked the door to Shannon's room around 5 o'clock. She was also freshly scrubbed, wearing a fluffy pink robe and matching slippers and carrying an armful of clothes and make-up.

Shannon had dried her hair and tied it back while she cleansed and moisturised her face. She watched Erin dump everything on her bed and gave her a questioning look.

"I know we're not exactly bosom buddies, Shannon, but beggars can't be choosers and since its ages since I got to get ready for a night out with one of the girls, I thought you'd do."

Shannon managed to smile.

"So, can I do your hair and make-up? I'm really good. All my friends used to let me do theirs. You got any music? No? Damn, hang on 'till I get some. We can't get ready without music. You want some Bacardi?"

Erin was gone before Shannon could answer and was back less than five minutes later with an ipod, two glasses, a bottle of Bacardi, hair straighteners and her sweet but alarming ability to talk for ages without taking a breath.

Shannon was charmed, slightly mystified and delighted as she found herself getting caught up in Erin's enthusiasm for their night out. Maybe it wouldn't be so bad to act like a normal woman for a change – a normal woman heading out to a club and flirting with an attractive man. She giggled as Erin pulled pot after pot of dark pink blusher from the pile on the bed and allowed herself to enjoy the experience. Maybe tonight would be fun.

****

Mitch stood in the corridor outside Shannon's room. He could hear the two girls giggling and chatting inside but couldn't quite bring himself to knock on the door and go in. He pressed two fingers to his temples – his head was pounding; this was a big night for them all and his mind wasn't as centred as he would've liked.

He'd spent the past week watching Matt and Shannon, trying to figure out what was going on, if anything. There had been nothing overt in their actions, a few stolen glances here and there, especially from Matt's direction but then he'd known since Donegal that Matt was attracted to Shannon. Despite what she'd told him, Shannon seemed to be keeping things professional. Maybe their little chat had convinced her to play it cool, surely she still trusted his judgement of people? He wasn't fool enough to think that her feelings for him had changed but that wasn't important right now. Was it?

Keeping her sweet was important, at least until things were settled and he had his money and position back. That's what was important, right? Christ he needed a pain killer. Or a drink.

Mitch turned away from the bedroom door and followed the stairs down to the kitchen where Sean was already making short work of another whiskey.

"One for you?" he asked as Mitch joined him at the table. Mitch nodded, the frown still etched onto his face. "Penny for 'em?" Sean studied his father's worried eyes.

"Ah, they're not even worth a penny, Sean," Mitch told him, taking a sip of his drink. "Just a lot to think about."

"Nerves?"

"Aye. We're so bloody close and I don't want anything to go wrong." He shook his head. "Maybe this whole night out carry on was a bad idea."

Sean frowned. "What do you mean? It gets you and Shannon among the people that matter and it's a good cover. What can go wrong?" He paused. "Carter?"

Mitch nodded. "I still just can't shake the feeling that it's a little too convenient, him showing up like that."

"If you weren't certain about him then you should've left him in Portstewart."

"I would've done but Shannon was bloody adamant about bringing him with us." He stroked his chin thoughtfully. "Now, why would she do that?"

"Picking up a good looking guy?"

"He looked like shite that first night."

"Maybe she just wanted another man around, someone to protect her from your flirtin'" Sean grinned but Mitch stiffened.

"Protection." Mitch said thoughtfully.

"Eh?" Sean screwed his face up trying to follow the train of thought.

Mitch pulled a phone from his pocket and tapped in a number. "Grace? Yeah, listen. I have an inkling that we're being played here. How quickly could you get some lads together? Yeah, I know but I don't want anything fucking this up so we should be ready. What? Well, I think that Shannon arranged for Matt Carter to be sent over here. I think she's trying to get back to Lewis Carter. No, I don't have any evidence; it's just a gut feeling. No, no, just have them ready in case Carter makes an attempt to extract her tonight. Yeah, you too." Michael closed the phone with a snap and turned to Sean just as Matt entered the kitchen, brushing some stray hairs from the jacket of his new suit.

He sensed the atmosphere immediately. Mitch was tense and Sean was trying to relax but failing miserably. Matt felt a moment's unease but brushed it aside. It would have been more worrying if Mitch wasn't tense. He sat himself down at the table.

"Any idea where exactly we're going tonight?"

Mitch composed himself with obvious difficulty. "Apparently we're having a Chinese and then heading to some fancy club. It'll likely be shite – all loud music and those bloody flashing lights. Give me a wee pub with a couple of guys jammin' any day."

Sean managed a laugh. "You sound like you're about ninety, Dad. The Warehouse is pretty good and it's members only so there won't be any arseholes."

Matt grinned. "Great, sounds like a good night."

Mitch glanced at his watch. "Go and tell the women to hurry on, Sean. We'll miss our table if we don't make a move here."

Sean left, glancing at his father, a look that Matt didn't miss. For a few moments there was silence in the kitchen. They heard Sean roaring up the stairs for Erin to pull on any old thing and hurry up 'cause he was 'starved'. Mitch swirled his whiskey around his glass and then downed it. Yep, he was definitely anxious about something. Matt decided that it was as good a time as any to dip his toe in the water and cause some ripples.

"Er…Mitch. I was wondering…"

Mitch scowled at him. "About what?"

"You and Shannon."

"Yeah?"

"Are you two still…I mean, I know that you still have feelings for her but I kind of got the impression that it was one-sided and I wanted to ask just in case I was wrong."

Mitch combed a hand through his hair. "Any particular reason why you want to know?"

Matt laughed self-consciously. "Come on, Mitch. She's gorgeous and I know that you've seen me noticing. If things are completely over between you two then I'd like to…um…"

Mitch's eyes narrowed. "Not that long ago you were drugged to the eyeballs and wanting to die because you missed your wife and child so much. Now you're telling me that you're in the mood to get some with my ex."

Matt forced himself to smile. "I admit that I was low for a long time but then I met Shannon and I realised that life goes on and there are people out there who've had experiences just as bad, if not worse, than mine and they don't hide in their apartments and try to drink themselves to oblivion."

"Helps that she's hot too, huh?"

Matt grinned. "Yeah."

Mitch stood up and nodded slowly. "So you're being all gentlemanly about the thing and asking before you dive in." Matt nodded. "And if I said that I'm not done with her?"

Matt frowned. "Sounds ominous but if that's how you feel then I'd have to step back."

Mitch raised his eyebrows. "Wow. What a decent human being you are, Matt Carter." Matt said nothing. "Well, let me put it to you like this; I am not finished with Shannon but I believe that she is finished with me. I could be wrong so I'll leave it up to you

– if you choose to make a move on her and get rejected then it'll be a damn pity and I'll be the first to buy you a pint to drown your sorrows in."

"And if I don't get rejected?"

"Then you should know that I'll do everything in my power to win her back."

Matt rubbed his face. "I don't want to get into a competition with you, Mitch."

"No?" Mitch laughed. "Well, I reckon you already are." He held out a hand. "Let the best man win?"

Matt shook Mitch's hand warily as Sean opened the kitchen door. He eyed their clasped hands. "Taxi's waiting and the girls are coming down."

Mitch nodded to Matt and headed into the hall, slinging a jacket over his shoulder as he went; Sean signalled for Matt to follow and closed the door behind them. Matt kept his head down, thinking back over the conversation, trying to figure out if he'd just made things worse or spiced things up. He was wondering if it would be safer all round to call things off when he heard Sean's sharp intake of breath. Matt looked up and his mouth fell open.

Shannon and Erin were coming downstairs with Erin just in front. She was wearing a tight, jade green oriental-style dress which seemed to Matt to end just a few inches below her waist and which clung to every curve of her voluptuous body. Sean gave a low, appreciative whistle and Erin's smile widened.

Shannon had opted for a short black skirt and a sparkling gold handkerchief top. Her dark hair was down and very straight, it looked like silk against her creamy skin. Her make-up, in contrast to Erin's, was light and natural with smoky dark eyes and creamy tan lipstick. She came down onto the last step and turned to face the door. Matt's breath caught in his throat. Her top was held together by two thin straps – one at the back of her neck and one at her waist, otherwise her back was naked. He followed the fall of her hair down to the dimple at the base of her spine and knew that Mitch's eyes were on him. Shannon looked back at him over her shoulder and the challenge in her eyes made him grin.

It was going to be a very long night.

Chapter Twenty

Matt surveyed the scene before him, The 'Warehouse Club' certainly lived up to its name – once the site of an old clothing manufacturer, it had been saved from dereliction almost three years ago and transformed into a thriving social enterprise.

Although open plan, the club operated successfully on three levels; on the top floor was the gaming level which was almost a small casino – roulette wheels, blackjack and immaculate card dealers in dark green waistcoats over white shirts – and was alive with both the serious and casual gamblers; the second floor was a drinker's heaven – a bar ran the width of the room and from there to the glass wall where he was now standing were tables, leather sofas and chairs, and a myriad of waiting staff; the basement level was a huge dance floor, heaving with bodies – Matt could look out over it from his position at the edge of the bar area. He had a good view of the wrought iron staircase that wound from one floor to another and the main door which was off to his left. Conversations around him were loud and often raucous, clashing with the yells from the gambling floor and the heavy beat of the music from the floor below. It shouldn't have worked but it was oddly enchanting and the fact that it seemed populated by flawless women only helped to make Matt feel right at home.

Tonight, however, his interest was only in one particular woman and she was currently dancing somewhere below him. Every now and again Matt made out a flash of gold that could have been her but he couldn't quite see through all the strobe lights and dry ice to be certain. Shannon, Erin and Sean had hit the dance floor about ten minutes ago and Sean had come back upstairs a few minutes later and visited some of the occupied tables, shaking hands and generally acting like a good host. Mitch had disappeared as soon as they'd come in and Matt couldn't see him anywhere. Damn. Without Mitch around there was no point in trying to make him jealous. What if the meeting had already taken place? What if the powers that be had already been persuaded and were currently arming up to take him out and drag Shannon off to oblivion?

Matt took a sip of his Guinness and scanned the bar again – still no Mitch. He turned back to the view of the dance floor and was ridiculously relieved to see Shannon and Erin climbing the stairs together, giggling and chatting. Shannon caught his gaze and her smile widened. Erin turned to see what she was smiling at and then leaned close to Shannon and whispered something. Shannon nodded and the two of them began giggling again. Matt shook his head but couldn't quite manage not to smile.

Shannon made her way to stand beside him and leaned back against the glass. "Phew. That was fun but I am SO out of shape."

Matt raised an eyebrow and looked her up and down. "You look okay to me," he said with a grin.

Shannon rolled her eyes. "That's your chat up line?" She shook her head, tutting. "Dreadful."

"Hey, I told you I was rusty. I'll improve." Matt told her.

She smiled up at him and leaned in a little closer. "Notice anything interesting?" she asked, chewing on her bottom lip.

"Even 'though you're trying very hard to distract me, yes, I've noticed that there are 2 exits on each floor and all of them are well guarded."

Shannon walked two fingers up his chest. "Yeah, the waiting staff who haven't moved to lift a glass once tonight."

Matt slipped an arm around her waist and leaned close, "Three tables back on the right, the large table on the back left and the tables on either side of the entrance to the rest rooms. Lots of heavy lookin' dudes."

Shannon threw back her head and laughed as though he'd said something hilarious. "Mitch and Grace have just joined Sean at the bar," she told him as she slipped her arms around his neck.

"Last chance to call this off," Matt told her, his mouth inches from her lips.

Shannon stood up on her tip-toes and laid her cheek against his. "I think the guys at the biggest table are the head honchos and I don't think Mitch has made his pitch yet, Grace has been instructing him on how to play it, what to say. Sean's been warming them up and pretty soon they'll all go over there and the introductions will be made."

Matt looked between Mitch and the big table as Shannon was talking. It made sense. "Ok, I'll buy that. What about all the heavies? You think there's as much armed muscle as this on a regular Friday night?"

Shannon leaned back a little to look into his face. She was smiling prettily. "You think all this is for our benefit? I'm touched."

Matt grinned at her and touched his forehead to hers. "You think it's all for the meet?"

"Maybe, maybe not. If it is then it would be kind of a shame to disappoint them, wouldn't it?" Shannon closed her eyes and tipped her head just a little; let her fingers dance across Matt's shoulders. "Maybe you should just kiss me and we'll see what happens?"

Matt grinned. "Only 'cause you asked real nice." He leaned forward but stopped abruptly.

Shannon frowned and turned to see where he was looking.

A waiter was standing beside them with a tray containing two champagne flutes. Shannon looked at Matt questioningly. "Nice touch but terrible timing," she told him.

Matt laughed. "Not my doing."

He nodded to the waiter who handed them a champagne flute each. "Compliments of the gentleman at the bar," he told them before gliding off back into the crowd.

Matt and Shannon turned around to see Mitch watching them. He lifted his own glass and raised it towards them. Matt did the same and turned back to Shannon. "He's not smiling," he said.

"Seems we have his attention," she told him, "Slow dances are starting; we should go and cause some more trouble."

"Yeah, I mean what can he do, shoot us?" Matt took a sip of his champagne and smiled in Mitch's direction.

"Very witty. You should be in entertainment," Shannon said with a throaty giggle.

A woman had walked up to stand in front of Mitch. She was small and blonde, wearing a conservative black dress and heels that weren't built for dancing. She spoke to Mitch briefly before looking back towards Matt and Shannon.

"That's Grace," Shannon told him, dropping her untouched drink onto the nearest table and taking his hand. "Ready to make your Dublin debut?" Matt grinned and drained his glass before following her to the stairs. He was starting to enjoy himself.

They walked down the staircase hand in hand and then stood for a moment as one song ended and another began. "I should probably have told you," Matt had to talk loudly so that Shannon could hear him over the music. She raised an eyebrow. "I don't dance," he finished with an embarrassed smile.

"Well, shuffle your feet and watch me then," Shannon pulled him onto the dance floor and began to move, gyrating slowly to the beat, swaying away from him and then back again. Matt shuffled, glancing around self-consciously. He saw Shannon's eyes dart to the glass wall upstairs and she immediately swayed forward to slip into his arms. "Mitch is watching," she told him a little breathlessly. "Maybe you should start with your seduction routine."

"Start? I had you eating out of my hand upstairs." Matt leaned against her a little – a wave of dizziness sweeping through him. He shook his head to clear it.

"No, sweetie it was the other way round. I had you falling at my feet. If that waiter hadn't arrived when he did you'd be trying to lead me into a dark corner to ravish me."

Matt hid a smile. "Sorry, were you saying something there? I was too busy staring at the ass of that blonde that just walked past."

Shannon punched him playfully on the arm and he laughed, pulling her close as Snow Patrol's 'Chasing Cars' boomed around the room. "Mitch still watching?" he asked.

Shannon moved him around a little so she could get a better view. "Yep. Have you made a move yet? You might want to warn me in case I miss it."

Matt grinned and trailed his fingers lightly across the bare skin of her back making her suck in her breath and arch against him. Her hands slid back around his neck and her fingers began to caress the sensitive area at the nape of his neck.

"Well?" She purred.

"Mmmmm." Matt breathed against her cheek and closed his eyes.

Shannon had hers closed too. She was leaning into his touch, loving the way his thumb was moving in slow circles at the base of her spine, the heat of his body against hers. She allowed her fingers to trace the breadth of his shoulders and slide down his chest. He leaned down and dropped a feather-light kiss onto her bare shoulder and she shivered and turned her head to face him.

Matt squeezed his eyes closed and open again. The feeling of dizziness and disorientation was growing and his limbs were beginning to feel heavy. Shannon had turned to face him, her lips parted slightly and her hands slid into his hair.

"I'm going to kiss you," Matt whispered to her with a grin.

Shannon barely had time to register what he'd said before his lips were on hers. His arms tightened around her and she melted against him, tasting him as he sighed into her mouth and she felt a tingle all the way to her toes. It was sweet and tender and full of promises that made her kiss him back and hold onto him just a little bit tighter. She broke off from the kiss and Matt swayed against her, shaking his head.

"You okay?" she asked. "Too much for you, am I?"

"Could be, you've definitely made my head spin." He grinned and shook his head again, pressing his knuckles against his eyes. He staggered a little and as Shannon pulled him upright, she looked around.

Sean was descending the stairs, dragging a very unhappy-looking Erin with him. Erin glanced up and caught Shannon's eye, grimacing as she tried to extricate herself from Sean's grip. Shannon frowned but as soon as they hit the floor, Erin and Sean were lost in the sea of people.

"Maybe I'm drunk," Matt was telling her. "I mean, it's been ages since I had any booze."

"What did you drink tonight?" Shannon asked him, helping him to lean against her.

"Um, I just had water with the meal, a Guinness when we

arrived here and the champagne from Mitch but that's all, I mean could I be this pissed on…?"

They both looked at each other.

Shannon looked around again and caught sight of Sean and Erin at the far side of the dance floor. They were obviously having quite a heated discussion, Erin was waggling a finger at Sean and he was dragging her towards an exit which was staffed by two angry looking bouncers.

"What is it?" Matt slurred.

"Well, Sean and Erin are having a bit of a domestic. Looks like he's trying to get her to leave before the action starts and she's having none of it." She glanced to their left. Some of the heavies had moved downstairs. At least three of them were between them and the downstairs exit. "And the goon squad is blocking our escape route," she told him. "What's going on?" she wondered aloud.

Matt was concentrating hard on keeping his balance. He couldn't seem to think clearly. "Damn," he whispered as it hit him. "They think I'm trying to get you out."

Shannon very clearly felt herself pale. She checked his pulse and looked into his heavy-lidded eyes. "Ok, racing pulse, dilated pupils, dizziness, slurred speech…so Mitch put something in your drink. We have to get out of here." She turned to move but Matt pulled her back.

"Symptoms…" he choked out.

"Huh?" Shannon was looking around frantically for some way to get them through the sea of people.

"Narolin."

She turned to look at him and Matt saw the moment that she realised. "No." she whispered and her eyes widened.

Matt nodded. "He used Narolin, which means that in a few minutes I'm going to pass out and it'll be up to forty-eight hours before this all wears off. You have to…"

"No." Shannon slung Matt's arm across her shoulders and began elbowing their way towards the right side of the club and the exit that Sean was still trying to steer Erin to. "Matt try to help me here. We can get out. I can…"

Matt was shaking his head. "In a few minutes you won't be able to carry me anymore. I'll be a dead weight." He swallowed and closed his eyes, concentrating on forming the words. "Even if we made it outside, I'd just slow you down. You have to leave me here and get in touch with dad."

"I am NOT leaving you," Shannon told him fiercely, glaring at a man on her left who had the audacity to laugh at 'the state of that drunk'. She was half dragging, half-carrying him, he was getting heavier with every step and why the hell couldn't people move out of the way? "I didn't leave you in Portstewart and I didn't even know you then. I'm sure as hell not leaving you now." Matt stumbled and she fought to keep both of them on their feet. "C'mon Matt, talk to me, stay awake. I can't do this on my own. Please." She felt fear bubble up inside her and fought against the hot tears that threatened to blur her vision. "Damn it."

"You're stronger than you think," Matt told her, his head sagging onto his chest. "Leave me and run. Find my Dad. Find Denton. Crush these bastards..." his voice trailed off and he dipped forward. Shannon put all of her effort into pulling Matt's slipping arm back onto her shoulder and then became acutely aware that the pressing surge of dancing bodies was thinning. Turning she saw Mitch coming slowly down the stairs, his eyes were fixed on her and the expression on his face was triumphant. The fake waiters that she'd spotted earlier were escorting people to the exits. No-one was looking back or protesting.

There was a final surge of people and Shannon found herself face to face with Erin who was looking around her like a frightened rabbit. "Get out of here now, Shannon. They want you. They won't touch him," she hissed before scurrying off into the fast receding crowd.

Matt groaned and his feet finally went from under him. Shannon tugged on his arm ineffectually and finally slid onto the floor beside him. Cradling his head in her lap she let the tears come as the club emptied around her and the music stopped. She dropped her head and placed a soft kiss on Matt's forehead. Decision time.

"I'll come and get you," she whispered and gently lowered his head to the floor.

Shannon stood up and looked around. The dance floor was ringed with figures carrying assault rifles and hand guns. On the third tier of the stairs, Mitch stood quietly watching her. Their gazes locked.

And then the lights went off.

Chapter Twenty-one

Shannon moved immediately, ducking low and heading towards the stage. There was the hiss of static somewhere close – a radio or walkie-talkie she presumed – and then the scuff of a shoe. She paused, waited and then felt her way to the edge of the stage. Reaching down she slipped off her heels and then swung herself up and into the recently-vacated dj booth. She waited.

Mitch's voice echoed around the building. "Come on now, sweetheart. No-one here wants to hurt you. We just want to talk to you, negotiate. Come on up here and we won't hurt lover boy. I promise."

Shannon ignored him. She breathed deeply, closing her eyes and concentrating on each breath to calm herself down. She focused on remembering all the exits, their placement on each of the floors, the number of out-of-place people that she and Matt had spotted. Matt. Her mind flew back to him and she had a sudden flash of day-dream – she was sitting in a garden reading a newspaper, to her left Matt was pushing their son on a swing and she smiled as their laughter filled her with a sense of peace and contentment. She swallowed hard. She might not like it but Matt and Erin were right – she had to get out of here, get help and then come aback fighting. It was just a matter of patience and calm.

"Your brother died squealin'," announced another voice and Shannon froze. "He was part of my payment for doin' the rest of 'em. After I was done with him I cut him open and licked his blood off my knife. He tasted goooood. I wonder if you taste as sweet. You got away from me that night, darlin', but it won't be happenin' again." Shannon's eyes snapped open and she had to fight to keep herself from running up there and scratching that man's eyes out. She reached out with her mind and found him, the foul stench of his soul filled her mind and she grimaced. He was telling the truth – this man, Blade they called him, had murdered her family. There was an acrid taste in her mouth and she bit back a retort. This was not the time. They were trying to distract her as they crept around and blind-sided her. It was time to move.

Up on the next floor Grace nudged Blade and took the megaphone from him. She switched it off. "Enough you maggot," she growled.

"Aw, c'mon Gracie. Ya told me to distract her." He grinned revealing a mouthful of nicotine-stained teeth.

"You enjoyed it just a bit too much," Mitch peeped over the table they had hunkered down behind.

They had a good view of the main part of the floor where Matt lay unmoving, the stage and the booth where Shannon had hidden – all of it was partially hidden in deep shadows but Mitch could see movement down both sides of the dance floor. The men were almost in position and they were drawing their weapons. He sneaked a glance at Grace, wondering how this had got out of hand so fast. One minute he was slaking his jealousy by sending spiked drinks to Shannon and Matt, the next the backers had made their decision – and it involved taking Shannon there and then – Grace had seen that their prize was getting much too close to the exit and the whole situation had taken on its own momentum.

Mitch could feel Grace's eyes on him. She knew that he was concerned about Shannon – that he was a bit soft when it came to her – and he knew that Grace was tough and callous, ready to do whatever it took to push things forward. He sighed. He couldn't really complain. He'd come to them with the proposition after all.

Grace motioned for him to hurry up. This was his last chance to end this peacefully and he knew it. The men were waiting.

Mitch flicked the switch on the megaphone. "Shannon?" His voice echoed around the empty club. "Let's not do this, sweetheart. You know it doesn't have to be like this – we can all come to an agreement. No-one has to get hurt. You and I are good together, princess. We make a good team and these guys need us. They're fighting a war here, Shannon. They've been fighting for almost thirty years and we can help them to win and to bring about a real lasting peace on this island. When that's done…" he swallowed. "…when that's done then you're free to go. Even if it's Matt that you choose to be with afterwards, I'll understand and respect your wishes."

Silence.

"What d'you say, princess?"

Silence.

Mitch moistened his dry lips with his tongue and reluctantly handed over the megaphone to Grace. She smiled at him and leaned forward to whisper, "She won't come, Michael. She was setting you up to fail tonight. She's the ringleader, not Carter. I heard it myself."

Mitch paled. "What? No. How?"

Grace smiled again. "I bugged the house, heard her cozying up to Carter to get him to put on a good show for you, turn your head so you'd screw everything up. And you did. Lucky for you, I'm here to save your ass. Again." She turned to the balaclava-clad man on her right and gave him the thumbs up. Blade was grinning at him too.

Mitch felt suddenly nauseous. He clutched at Grace's arm as she got up to go. "Don't hurt her, Grace." He whispered.

Grace stood for a moment looking down at him and then she sighed and knelt down, leaning close to his ear. "If she won't agree to what we want then I'll have no option, Michael. We've wasted enough time and energy on this, at your insistence. Well, the softly, softly approach didn't work did it? Time to do it my way." She moved to stand up. Mitch grabbed her arm again.

"And Matt Carter?"

Grace shrugged. "He could be useful if she tries to get back to Lewis Carter. Otherwise he's expendable."

Mitch let go of her arm and sat down heavily. He had always known that there was a possibility things wouldn't end well but he wasn't ready to give up yet. A hero's welcome home was a few breaths away – he could have it yet. So long as Shannon didn't do anything stupid.

****

Shannon had crawled through the dark to the back of the stage and was sitting on her knees with her hands extended in front of her, as though they were pressing on an invisible wall. She felt calm and back in control, focused on the energy flowing around her hands and the pictures flowing into her mind as she read the space in front of her and found the men who were waiting in the darkness.

Her head twitched as there was the soft whisper of static – a radio she thought – and a man on her left began to walk forward, his gun held in front of him in both hands. He walked slowly, taking great care to place his feet gently on the wooden boards. A stair on the other side of the stage creaked as the right flank began to move too. Shannon concentrated on breathing deeply – air into her lungs, air out – as she gathered energy from the dark, waiting warehouse.

They were descending the main stairs when Mitch heard it and stopped. The others came to a halt too, looking about in confusion as the whistling, hissing noise rose around them. Mitch turned to shout a warning to the men at the front of the dance floor but his gathered breath was sucked from him as Shannon pulled more and more power into her mind.

The pull of it brought her to her feet and she fought to control it until she was ready, until the men were closer. The taste of it made her lick her lips in anticipation and then the first man made it to the booth in front of her and she knew that the time had come.

She yelled as she released it and the men advancing on her were hurled across the bottom floor of the club, smashing into the back wall with a sickening crunch and finally falling into a heap on the dance floor. None of them moved again. Shannon wasn't finished. She thrust her arms out, walking forward and driving the rest of the energy in front of her. The glass wall smashed and blew across the bar, mirrors, champagne flutes, high balls, bottles, every light bulb and window in the club smashed and every man and woman still in the building was hurled to the floor.

For a few seconds there was a shocked silence and then shaky figures began to stand up, shake glass off themselves, call for help. Grace pulled herself from under a chair and stood up. Mitch was already standing and looking across at the stage. Shadows whirled and bulged as the back-up men searched.

Grace was smiling when he turned to her. "You were right," she told him. "The things we could do with that weapon at our disposal."

Mitch opened his mouth to respond but there was a shout from the men before he could. "She's gone."

"It's over," Mitch said despondently. "She won't come back."

Grace shook her head. "Grow a set, Michael. We have Matt Carter and she'll come back for him."

"I wouldn't." Mitch told her.

"No, but you're not falling for him, are you?" She walked into the middle of the devastation, pulling a shard of glass from her leg as she went. "My God, she's incredible. We have to have her," she was mumbling.

Mitch was frowning. "I didn't know that she could do that," he whispered.

****

Shannon was shivering with cold. Her meagre clothing had been perfect for dancing in Matt's arms but it was no protection for the heavy Dublin rain. Added to the fact that she now had no shoes, Shannon knew that she was in a mess. She also knew that she couldn't leave yet. She had to know that Matt was okay.

She was flattened against a huge black bin, at the far end of the wide alley behind the club, when the first of them came out. Guns raised, eyes darting everywhere, three of the non-waiters led Grace, Mitch and Blade out of the back door and towards waiting cars. Three men followed carrying Matt between them with another two men bringing up the rear. She shrank as far back as she could, easing into the shadows between the dumpster and the wall.

Staying in shadow, Shannon slipped a little closer. Her teeth were chattering and her legs were shaking – from cold and the after effects of directing so much energy through her body. She squinted through the rain, willing some one of them to disclose some valuable titbit of information and praying that they wouldn't harm Matt. Their exit from the club and into the dark night took less than a minute and no-one spoke. Damn.

Shannon slid slowly down the wall. Her head was pounding and her eyelids were starting to feel very heavy. She needed to rest. The wall bit into her naked back and the rain soaked into her already sodden clothes. She looked around for some inspiration but the alley offered her nothing but empty beer bottles and a week's worth of spoiling food, and the rain gave no sign of stopping anytime soon. She needed to find shelter.

Shannon pulled herself to her feet and limped back towards the back door of the club. Miraculously it was still open and she slipped cautiously inside, all her senses on alert in case someone had been left behind. Inside was pitch black and she waited for a few seconds after the door had thumped shut for someone to come out of the dark and grab her.

The cavernous space stayed silent and Shannon made her way carefully back to the stage, avoiding as much broken glass as she could and cursing her lack of shoes as the odd glass shard bit into her skin. At the stairs to the stage, she sank to the floor. She no longer had sufficient strength to keep moving and so she sat still for a moment, her head in her hands and her eyes closed.

This was the downside of such spectacular shows of power – like a hangover after a particularly good night out. Her arms felt like lead and the rest of her body seemed to slowly be turning to unresponsive stone. She let her head slide onto the next stair riser and allowed herself to cry. This was her fault. She should've told Denton to come and get them. To hell with being a heroine and to hell with helping Lewis Carter snap up a few dozen terrorists. She could be safe and warm in a hotel bed by now. Matt could be safe and warm in a hotel bed too. They could be safe and warm in the same hotel bed.

Shannon grinned at that. She couldn't stay here, someone would come back soon – maybe even the Gardai – and she couldn't afford to be locked up when Matt was in trouble. She was the only one who could help him right now.

Matt wouldn't be sitting here feeling sorry for himself, she told herself. If Matt was here he would be pulling himself together and hunting them down.

And Blade was with them. Blade who had murdered her family. Blade who had taken a young boy from his home, terrified and alone, and killed him. Her brother. Her David.

Shannon pushed herself slowly back into a sitting position and focused on Blade. Anger burned in her throat. Tears threatened again and she blinked furiously. The time to feel defeated and emotional was over. She just needed to think. Or maybe catch a lucky break.

Shannon looked out across the club and ran through her options – she needed to find her shoes, she needed to find some money, then a call box to contact Denton. She needed to sleep but that would have to wait. All she had at the minute were the clothes on her back. She pulled on the hem of her soaking gold top. She needed to find clothes that didn't make her look like a hooker.

At the far side of the dance floor a small light shone in the deep shadows. She'd been staring at it without seeing it for almost ten minutes. Frowning, Shannon rose to her feet. Her legs wobbled but she forced herself to stay standing. Inch by inch she moved through the suffocating darkness, her feet crunching on debris and her head swimming alarmingly. By the time she reached it, Shannon was whimpering at the pain of a thumping headache and badly lacerated feet.

She reached down and clutched it in her hand as her vision swam and her legs threatened to give way. Shannon drew in a lungful of air and steadied herself before bringing the device close to her face. It was a clamshell phone – one of the men she'd blasted must've dropped it.

Shannon grinned. As lucky breaks went this one was pretty close to miraculous.

For a few moments her brain wouldn't work – the simple act of remembering Denton's phone number was suddenly too much to do. She wanted to cry with frustration but she didn't have the energy. Cursing, Shannon flipped open the phone and concentrated as hard as she could. The numbers flowed into her mind and she tapped them in frantically.

Denton answered on the third ring. He sounded groggy. "Hello? This is not a good time, 'unknown caller' so this better be an emergency."

""Dent," gasped Shannon.

"Who is this?" Denton was immediately alert.

"My designation is…um, my authorisation is…" Shannon gulped back a sob. "Designation Stargate, authorisation 4479865240," she whispered.

"Continue." Dent said, his voice low and urgent. She could hear him moving around.

"They have Matt, he'll be needing an extraction. Let Lewis know. It's all my fault, Dent. I thought Mitch wouldn't figure it out, thought I could offer them up instead of me but I just got him hurt. Tell Lewis I just wanted to be a normal…" Her voice trailed off as exhaustion won and she hit the floor with a thud that echoed through the empty building.

Chapter Twenty-two

The room in Ballykelly was buzzing – everyone seemed to be shouting into phones, tapping hard on computer keyboards or running back and forth waving sheets of information. It was almost 2 in the morning.

Shannon's phone call had turned their little operation on its head almost an hour ago and since then everyone had gone into overdrive. The Intel from the group on the ground wasn't happy news. The car containing Mitch Cooper, Grace Connor, Blade and Matt hadn't gone back to Sean's house. It had been lost among the back streets of Dublin. Shannon had been picked up and was on her way north.

Lewis was pacing and chewing his finger nails. Marilyn would kill him when he got home. Denton said nothing. He figured Lewis had more important things on his mind than healthy nail beds. And Marilyn would understand about it all once she heard about Matt. Because they would get Matt back and home safely to his mother. Denton had faith in that.

The outer door opened and Frank came in. He took off his shades and shook rain from his jacket. He was in swat gear, still pumped up from their raid. Lewis looked up and nodded for his report.

"Brian Nelson, age 32. Sympathiser and very in with the top brass. We hit the right dude anyway." Frank told him.

Lewis nodded. "Did he spill any info?"

Frank grinned. "Eventually. The pin is Grace Connor, like you thought. Apparently there's dissent in the ranks about the way she's handling things. Some of them think it's time to forget about diplomacy and plant a few bombs, cut a few throats."

"So someone's looking to take Grace out?"

"Yep, although the word in their sick little grapevine is that Grace has found herself a real prize – some major shit super weapon – and so, for the minute, everything's up in the air until the pretender to the throne finds out what it is and if she really has it or if she's bullshitting them all."

"Any thoughts on the pretender?" Denton asked.

Frank shrugged. "Our boy wasn't giving that up. He's scared of whoever it is." Lewis was pacing again. "Logic would suggest that it's Blade. He's a scary type of guy."

"Do I hear a 'but' coming?" Denton sat down in his chair and twirled his pen around like a baton – it helped him think.

Lewis nodded. His brow was furrowed in concentration. "Blade's old, Dent. Why wait until now to take over? I mean, he has the background for it and he's certainly bloodthirsty but…"

"Maybe that's exactly why, Sir." Interrupted Frank. Lewis glared at him for the distraction to his thought processes and then raised an eyebrow. "Well, it's like you said, Sir. He's old. What he might see as his glory days are behind him and he wants them again. He knows he's not getting any younger and Grace's leadership, although it's been successful and it's given the movement stability and a pretty high level of prosperity, it hasn't been high profile or savage."

Lewis cocked his head at Frank and grinned. "I always knew I kept you around for a reason, Frank."

Frank saluted stiffly. "Yes, Sir," he said loudly. "Permission to change, Sir?"

Lewis nodded. "Permission granted, soldier. Get a few hours' sleep and then get your ass back here, Frank. We're going to need you."

Frank saluted again and headed back out.

"Sir?" A call came from a young woman on the back row. She was holding a telephone. Lewis gave her a sharp nod.

"Group two has eyes on the secondarys."

"Sean and Erin," Denton said, throwing his pen in the air and catching it.

"Yes Sir. Secondarys are leaving the area. Group two is awaiting orders."

Lewis stopped pacing and folded his arms. "They're regrouping," he said, almost to himself. "Of course they are. They still have Matt."

Denton nodded. "He's bait." He looked up at Carter. "Bait for you?"

Lewis shook his head. "No, they think they still have a shot with Shannon. They think having Matt will lure her back to them." He looked up at the back row. "Have group two follow the secondarys at a distance. And keep us posted."

"Yes, Sir," she spoke urgently into the phone and then sat down and typed all the current intelligence into her computer. It came up on the main screen in front of them as a part of the on-going timeline. Lewis walked over and wrote it onto his board.

Denton sighed. "It's already on the computer screen, Lewis. Why do you need to write it up there too?"

Carter looked around at him and made a face. "God, you're cranky when you don't get a full night's sleep aren't you?" Denton rolled his eyes and said nothing. A retort was unnecessary. Carter sat down heavily in his chair and rubbed his eyes. He was trying not to think about Matt – his son could take care of himself. At least he used to be able to, but it had been a long time. "Dent? Did I make a mistake?" he asked softly.

Denton looked up at him and sighed. "No, Sir. You did not. A wise man once told me that decisions made at the beginning of a war should never be revisited at the end. Picking over actions already made serves no purpose other than to undermine your confidence in your ability to rationalise tough choices and make the best of the options open to you."

Lewis managed a weak smile. "I do tend to pontificate a lot, don't I?"

Denton nodded. "I blame being in congress, Sir."

Lewis nodded. "Some of my views aren't very popular, y'know."

Denton clasped a hand to his heart and made a face. "I'm shocked."

"Smartass."

Denton grinned and then was serious again. "Matt will come home, Lewis. Safe and sound."

Lewis nodded slowly and went back to staring at his board.

****

Matt woke sometime after midnight two days later. He ached from the top of his head to the tips of his toes. His tongue was stuck to the roof of his mouth and when he finally succeeded in un-sticking it, he could taste blood.

He sat up and rubbed his eyes. They felt hot and feverish. His head ached. He swung his legs off the bed and, wincing, stood up. He was still wearing the shirt and boxers that he'd worn to the club. And just like that it all came back to him. He was suddenly alert, bouncing onto his toes and scanning the room.

Erin was asleep in the easy chair by the window, her hands folded on her belly. He crept slowly up beside her and slid his hand over her mouth. She jumped, eyes wide, and made a low mewling sound in her throat as he pushed her back into the chair. He leaned in close, his mouth against her ear.

"When I take my hand away you're not going to scream are you?" he asked, his voice a low menacing growl. Erin shook her head. "I'm going to ask you some questions, that's all. I don't want to hurt you but I'm seriously pissed off just now and I will if I have to. Do you understand?" She nodded again, eyes wide.

Matt slid back a little and slowly took his hand away. Erin sat very still, watching him closely. She swallowed. Matt took a deep breath and rubbed his eyes again.

"It won't wear off properly until morning," Erin whispered. "You weren't supposed to wake till at least lunchtime."

Matt looked at her under his brows. "What time is it, Erin?" he asked, rocking back onto his heels and standing up. "And where the hell are we?" He moved away from her to sit on the end of the bed.

Erin relaxed a little and checked her watch. "It's twelve seventeen and before you ask it's Wednesday. We're in Sligo."

Matt hung his head. "Shit. And Shannon?"

Erin shrugged and tried to look nonchalant. "She's smart. She almost lost it back at the club when you dropped at her feet but she hasn't missed a beat since."

Matt allowed that to sink in. He cocked his head and looked at Erin for a moment, really looked at her. Erin swallowed but didn't look away.

"You know what I think?" Matt asked, leaning forward just a little, "I think you tried to help her. Why would you do that?"

Erin grimaced and began chewing on a nail. She stood up and turned away from him, walking over to the window and pulling the cord to angle the blinds so that she could see out. Two doors down a man was wheeling his bin to the edge of the pavement for the next morning's collection. A woman was just getting back from a late jog, pausing half-way through her garden to start her stretching and wind down. The odd car passed at the end of the road. It was late night for some, early morning for others but the street was still full of life. "It all looks so normal doesn't it?" she said finally. "We shouldn't be here among these normal people. We're not normal. We're evil. We've dealt in death and destruction and we're always thinking about doing it again. We decide who, where, when, even why. These people..." she indicated outside with a sweep of her arm, "...these people don't care about some ancient glorious cause anymore. They just want to live their lives," she turned back to Matt and her eyes were shining with tears.

"I was brought up to be a good girl, to go to mass, confess my sins, and look after the men in the family. My mother taught me all that. When she died I went to live with my grand-father and things, well, things were different. I still went to mass, still made my confession, still looked after the men in my family but I wasn't a good girl any longer. I flirted with my first soldier when I was sixteen, brought him back to a hotel and stood in the hall while they beat him to a pulp. My grandfather taught me to kill." She sighed; spread her hands palm up in front of him. "You can't see it, but I have blood on my hands."

"And your dad?" asked Matt.

Erin shook her head, still looking at her hands. "He was caught smuggling arms across the border and got four years. He was out in two but by then his face was known and he was a target. He was shot on his way to a meeting in the pub when I was six. They called him a hero, a martyr." She frowned and looked up at him. "He was just my dad and he was dead. I didn't understand."

"I'm sorry, "Matt said gently, reaching for her hand but she turned away again.

"I don't want your pity, Matt Carson, or your sympathy. I told you so that you'd understand. The world that I was born into hasn't given me anything but fear and pain. The rest of the universe has moved on and I want to as well. I don't want to be a part of this anymore." She knelt down until her eyes were level with Matt's, her hands on his knees. "I may not be the sharpest tool in the shed, Matt, but I think that you and Shannon can get me out."

Matt looked at her. It was a good story, well told. Maybe even plausible. He was, however, a cautious man with a suspicious mind and a newly acquired distrust of Mitch Connor. Holding her eyes with his he lifted her hands off his knees, eased her back away from him and made his decision.

"I came to Ireland because I felt that I owed my Dad. That's the simple truth. Beyond that I was to tell some heiress that a bunch of nasty people were after her for some reason, that they'd already taken out her contacts and that she was next. That's it. That was all I had to do. I didn't plan beyond that." Matt shook his head and studied his hands. "And now here I am getting mixed up with some crazy shit that I never wanted to get back into, getting my champagne spiked by my so called friend and finding out things about my dad and his history that, well, that I really didn't want to know. There's no master plan, Erin, no out at the end of it all, no pat on the back from the powers that be. This is all off the record and under the radar. I'm on my own." He looked up at her. "Sorry, Erin, you got the wrong guy."

For a moment Erin said nothing, just looked at him, her eyes wide and her face pale. Then she slowly sank to her knees and, with a wail of frustration, began to cry.

****

Matt woke in darkness. They had sedated him again before they moved him in case he gave them any trouble and now his body was stiff and sore from eighteen hours spent on a hard floor. His arms were bound securely at the wrists and elbows, his legs at the ankles and knees. More than anything he wanted to stretch a little to ease his aching muscles and try to figure out if there was any damage other than a few bruises and a touch of nausea. He tried to remain motionless, trying to get his bearings in the pitch black and figure out if he was alone.

A muffled snore from somewhere in the room confirmed that he had been right to be cautious. Not only was he trussed up like a thanksgiving turkey but he also had a guard. Matt took a moment to feel flattered and then slowly began to rotate each hand and foot in turn, returning feeling to his extremities but also producing an attack of killer pins and needles. He grimaced through the pain until he was satisfied that blood was flowing normally again and his limbs would obey him if he got the chance to use them.

He closed his eyes again, there was nothing to see anyway and the thick blackness all around him was disorientating. He tried to use his other senses to figure out where he was and who was with him. The floor beneath him was earth, with some small stones thrown in for good measure. He could feel several of them digging into his back. He could smell recently smoked cigarettes, after shave and the damp, stale air of a cellar. Somewhere close by there was a low creak and a brief exhalation as his companion turned over in his sleep.

Matt estimated that he lay there for almost an hour, rotating his hands and feet from time to time and listening to the changes in his jailer's breathing. Finally the mystery man woke up. After a bout of coughing, he rose from whatever bed he'd slept on and shuffled six steps towards Matt. There was the scratch and hiss of a match being lit and then a few seconds of silence when, Matt assumed, the man stood over him to check for any sign that he had begun to wake. Matt kept his breathing regular and the figure shuffled off again, twelve steps this time. As the figure moved away, Matt opened his eyes a fraction and looked around. The glow of the match was fading but he was able to see the outline of a low cot in the corner and rough wooden stairs leading up to a heavy looking dark wood door.

The man on the stairs swore as the match fizzed out, burning his fingers, then Matt heard the rasping sound of fingers on the wall as he felt his way to the steps, three dull thuds as he climbed them and then knocked on the door at the top. There was a pause and the door swung open. Matt closed his eyes against the sudden bright light but not before he saw Sean's silhouette in the doorway.

Matt waited until the muffled voices from upstairs drifted away and then he swung his legs around in front of him. Having them tied at the knees made it hard work to move but he managed to half-bounce, half-slide across to the area where he had seen the small cot. He bumped it with his feet and maneuvered himself around until he could reach it with his hands. Perhaps there was a sharp edge or a forgotten nail that he could use on the ropes. Listening intently for a noise from upstairs, he felt his way around the bed, first one way and then the other. Nothing.

"Shit!" he whispered.

Another match flared in the direction that he'd come from and he froze.

Mitch lit a cigarette, watching Matt through the flame and then blew the match out. The tip glowed dark red as he inhaled and Matt dropped his head. He'd been careful, but not careful enough.

"Mornin', Matt," said Mitch cheerfully. "We were beginning to wonder if our prize would ever wake up. Maybe I gave you a wee bit too much of the old Narolin. I never was much good with proper doses and all that malarkey. How do you feel?"

Matt did his best to grin into the darkness. "Oh, you know. Crap. Maybe if the ropes were off I'd feel better." Matt raised his eyebrows even though he knew Mitch couldn't see him.

Mitch laughed softly. "Always the joker, aren't you? Well, jokes on you this time, pal. The lovely Shannon left us to it. Or rather left you. That's a shocker, isn't it? She was always going to leave me sooner or later but you? I bet she made you feel real special. Her knight in shining armour, come all the way across the ocean to save her. I bet she was sooo grateful, told you how great things would be once you'd ditched me. Newsflash, Matt, Shannon is only interested in Shannon. The rest of us are collateral damage, to be used and then discarded as required."

Matt sighed. "You were the one who fucked things up there, Mitch. You sold her out."

"She told you that? You two really did get cozy didn't you?" Matt felt Mitch's breath close to his ear. "You can tell me now, Matt. I don't care anymore but I'm curious…did you screw her in the North or the South?"

Matt let the silence hang. He wanted to tell him the truth but he also wanted to keep him on edge. So he grinned instead. Mitch backhanded him across the jaw and scowled furiously.

Matt allowed himself a smile of triumph – one mission accomplished.

Chapter Twenty-three

The meeting place was a field just south of Strabane, near the border between Southern and Northern Ireland. Shannon stood by herself watching the helicopter descend. She was aware of the soldiers somewhere behind her, of the advance team of agents securing the perimeter, of the vague shapes drifting through the trees beyond the landing area as men patrolled all the access routes and possible sniper positions. She was acutely aware that she was an outsider here, and a woman. She had no idea which was the bigger problem.

The blades on the copter were impossibly large, slicing through the air, stirring up loose leaves and grasses and whipping her hair around her face. They continued to spin as Lewis Carter and three other agents jumped out and ran towards her, then the pilot lifted the huge machine smoothly off the ground again and it was gone.

Lewis stood in front of her and for a few moments they regarded each other.

He was a tall man, his almost-white hair and lined face only adding to his air of authority and control. His shoulders were broad, his hands large and tanned. He looked capable. She looked into his face and saw Matt there immediately. It was in the eyes, the line of the jaw, the hint of a dimple in the chin and the almost shy smile. She smiled back and held out her hand.

"Good to see you again, Sir," she said.

He shook her hand and nodded, gesturing for her to walk with him. The agents in his personal squad stayed at a respectful but watchful distance. Shannon saw a dark blue Vectra pull into the lane and a tall man in aviator sunglasses got out and stood with his back to them.

"So," Lewis began, "You know I want you along for the ride?" He didn't look at her but felt her bristle. "I know that's not what you would like but I think we need you. I think that Matt may need you." He glanced at her for a reaction, got none and sighed. He stopped walking. "I'm sorry that was…"

"Beneath you." she finished for him. Her eyes flashing fury and her face hard with distrust.

They had walked to within a few feet of the Vectra. Lewis looked at her. His brown eyes were steady. "That was the plan." He said. "Any operative we sent along would be in danger of Mitch shooting them on sight, of getting left behind in some way or another. With Mitch and Matt knowing each other the chances of that happening were slimmer. Plus we figured that you would want any link to us, no matter how tenuous, to be kept alive and to be kept close. I figured that when you found out that he was my son, you would know how seriously I took this."

Shannon's eyes were wide. "And if Mitch had just shot him?"

Lewis chewed on his lip. "Shit happens." he said and walked quickly to the car.

Shannon stood there for a few seconds, trying to force some steel into her spine again. She couldn't make up her mind whether Lewis Carter was incredibly clever or incredibly heartless. She shook herself and followed Lewis to the car where the Tom Cruise wannabe was holding the back door open for her. As she slid inside she earned herself a moment's contemplation from behind the sunglasses before he closed the door.

"So, what have you done?" she asked, her tone brisk and business-like.

Lewis allowed himself a small grin. "I've involved the local police and army, didn't want to make a mess if things get nasty and shots get fired."

"So this op is on the radar now?" Shannon was frowning.

Lewis nodded. "Unfortunately, yes. Couldn't be avoided. I'm hoping it's all kept low key enough to stay off the airwaves until we can nail them. We've been lucky. The help we've been given has been cleverly done. We've been allocated a house on one of the local bases in Ballykelly; it's a quiet location at the back, close to an exit and away from most prying eyes. We've set up a central command on the base and we're also getting a mobile unit underway. It's been circulated that this is a training exercise – war against terrorism and all that." He glanced at her and she smiled. "We've organised cover through a local firm and borrowed a van from them. I took the liberty of organising an advance party for you to lead. This is a multi-agency team, good men that I trust."

Shannon nodded. "And do they trust me?" she asked.

"They will if I tell them to." Lewis frowned. "You're valuable property, Shannon, but so is the president. No one agency is totally aware of your current capabilities but we're willing to assume that they've increased as you've matured. That's what your profilers led us to believe anyway and evidence from Andy Graham and his team seemed to support that before…" he looked away.

"It's okay." Shannon assured him. "Matt told me what happened. Who was it? Who wiped them all out?"

Lewis frowned. "We believe it was members of the group that Sean runs. Perhaps not on Sean's orders – there's no direct evidence of that."

"Then who?"

"Blade."

Shannon took a deep breath, let it out slowly. "I was in the same room as him. I could've…"

"No, you couldn't. We want them all, Shannon. Not just one. If you'd taken him out then you and Matt would both be dead and the rest of the group would be scattered to the four winds"

Shannon looked down at her hands, she knew that he was right but there was a bitter taste in her mouth and a deep sense of failure all the same.

"Anyway," Lewis went on. "We had to assume that if they were able to subdue you, make you work for them, that you would then be considered a clear and present danger to the well-being of our chief and, therefore, all agencies had to be involved. It's not the way I would've liked to handle it and probably not the best way to deal with it but it's necessary."

Conversation stilled as Lewis sat back and rubbed his eyes. Shannon looked around the car. It was clean to the point of obsession, with tinted windows and richly padded seats. There was a compact arrangement of drawers built into the pull down arm rest which held a phone, a notebook sized lap top and a compact digital camera. Shannon looked at it with a puzzled frown.

Lewis grinned. "I make sure I bring a camera with me everywhere I go,"he explained."My wife calls it an obsession but I just think you never know when you'll come across a photo opportunity. Much further Frank?"

"About ten minutes, Sir," Shades said from the front seat.

Shannon was trying to think of the best way to say what she wanted to tell him. She decided that direct was best.

"When you go back to the states?" she began."I won't be going with you. I want to see the end of this but then I'm gone."

Lewis looked across at her but she was staring straight ahead and her expression was hard to read. He sighed and cocked his head to the side, considering his response. "I won't say I hadn't anticipated this," he said gently,"I know that we did a lot of things wrong when you first came to us. We were so busy being overawed with your ability that somewhere along the line we forgot that you were still just a little girl, and a little girl who had lost her family."

"I saw counsellors. You thought of that," Shannon's voice was very quiet, measured, controlled.

"Yes, yes we did. And that was all well and good but what you really needed was stability for a while. What I did when you turned eighteen? I should've done that at the very beginning. You should've had a life first. Everyone was so excited by what you could do. Everyone wanted a part of you. You had people coming at you from all sides, all these agencies competing for your time and your energy, all wanting you to perform. We should've realised what that was doing to you."

"I hated you," Shannon said softly. "Every last one of you. "She turned to look at him."You all thought you knew everything about me, all those tests, all those hours doing the same things over and over and over. You knew nothing. I threw you crumbs and watched you all caper around with big smiles on your faces and fear in your eyes. I kept my secrets. And then when I finally got what I wanted - when I got my freedom? I realised that I couldn't be a normal person because no-one ever showed me how. I'll never be safe, never live in a normal house with a husband and children. I'll never have a yard with a dog and an apple tree. This'll never end for me." She laughed and it was the saddest sound that Lewis Carter had ever heard. "You want to know what else? Just now I realize that you're a fucking genius. You sent your son into a potentially explosive situation, he hadn't had combat experience of any kind for years, he's still carrying around a shit load of guilt over the death of his family and he almost died finding me…you sent him and Mitch spent hours analysing the reasons behind it. In the end it was all so simple."

Lewis chewed on his lip. The car was pulling into the army base.

"You sent him not because we already had a connection but because you knew that I'd see a kindred soul in him. You could kill two birds with one stone because Mitch would tell me who he was, Matt would find a reason to crawl back to reality and I'd know you were on my side. Matt was bait from the very beginning; you could see how it would be. You knew Mitch's personality, you knew that Matt needed someone that he could 'save' and thanks to those wonderful counsellors of yours you knew what I needed too. You're a brilliant strategist, Sir. I never realised until this minute just how good you are but you missed something."

She was close to tears. "What did I miss?" Lewis asked.

"You missed the fact that I grew up."

He looked at her blankly. "I don't understand."

"I grew up and I realised how different I was. I'm a freak of nature, Sir. I grew up suspicious and distrustful. I have few friends and no close friends and I don't socialise if I can help it. I hardly sleep. I jog at least four miles as many nights as I can manage it. I drink more than I should and I view every person I come into contact with as a potential threat." She paused and leaned towards him. "I only feel alive when I'm working, when I'm hunting someone, when I connect with them and share their thoughts. You did that to me and meeting Matt doesn't change that. It just makes me feel it even more keenly. He lost his family because of his work and I'll never have a family because of mine. At least he knew what it felt like to hold his daughter, to kiss his wife." She swallowed and looked down at her hands, feeling a tear slide down her cheek. "He hasn't drawn me back to the fold, Sir. He made me realise how you poisoned me and how much you're willing to risk to have my gift at your disposal again. Your son could've died…"

"No! I knew that you could protect him, that you would keep him safe. Like I told you before, I've made mistakes and not just with you. I feel my own mortality every day in a thousand different ways and it makes me realise what I've missed with my family, what I need to make up for. The pressures I put on my children, and my charges, to be what I wanted or needed them to be, not what they wanted or needed. I want to take my son home to his mother, alive and well." He sighed. "Yes, when I started all this I wanted you back. Not as a far flung contact who did the odd job for us but as an operative again. When we verified what Mitch was doing, what you suspected, and as time went on, well, I started to realise that the world has changed and my place in it isn't what I want it to be anymore. We never had much of a softly, softly approach but there seems to be an even greater need now for America to be strong, powerful, capable, even if the ways and means that are used to achieve that aren't always…right. It's a new kind of power struggle and, well, it scares the hell outta me."

Shannon shook her head. "It doesn't matter how noble your reasons for wanting me back are, Sir. I'm not coming. I'll do what I have to do to finish this and then I'm gone. If you try to take me by force, I'll fight you with everything I've got." She looked at him and he felt a shiver slide down his back. "I could kill you all if I had to." She looked away again and started chewing her nails.

Lewis sat back in his seat. Frank was out of the car and scouting around before he opened his boss's door. Lewis looked around without seeing much. He thought about the wrangling he'd had to do to get here in person, the expectations on him, the laws that he'd lived by and for during the last fifty odd years.

"For every action there is an equal and opposite reaction," he said.

Shannon looked at him. "What?"

"It's a law of physics. Every time I've been in a situation that requires a tough decision, I've thought about that law, it's kind of been my guideline. I think about the aftershocks, the casualties, possible pros and cons. I work it all out in my head. And in this case…" he paused.

"And in this case?" Shannon prompted.

"If I let you go, I'll be finished in Washington."

"Yes, you would."

"No agency would have me, not even as a consultant."

"You're supposed to be retired, Sir."

"I'd be a failure."

"Not to the people that matter."

"I would've let my president down."

"How?" Shannon frowned at him.

"You would still be a possible danger to him. For as long as you're not directly under the control of any agency, you're a loose cannon, a definite threat. If you were ever used against the president or against my country, I'd never forgive myself."

Shannon chewed on her lip and then smiled. "There is a solution."

Chapter Twenty-four

Sean came for him some time later, just as the sun had gone down and the sea had turned a deep purple. He steadfastly ignored all of Matt's questions until he had strapped him into a primitive wheelchair and wheeled him into one of the rooms off the corridor that Grace had pushed him up that morning.

'Dad'll take you for a piss in a minute. I'm just to leave you here.' Sean left, switching on the light before closing the door.

Matt blinked and looked around with a sinking heart.

The room was small and windowless. It was completely empty of furniture and everything – walls, ceiling and floor – was painted a glossy white. Sean had positioned the wheelchair on top of a large square of heavy plastic. Matt took a deep breath and sighed. The gloss paint made for easy cleaning; the colour made it easy to spot stains, the plastic was to collect any large spills. It was like a section from a terrorist training manual. "Chapter One: How to prepare An Interrogation Suite".

Matt tried to concentrate on his breathing. It was one of the first things they were taught - To be in control of the situation, you first have to control yourself. Knowing that you were about to be tortured was not conducive to a clear and practical mind. He needed to calm his breathing, focus his thoughts.

Behind him the door opened and Matt knew without looking who it would be. It was like a well-rehearsed script.

"Can I have a piss now, Mitch?" his voice tinged with more than a hint of sarcasm.

A column of cold steel pressed against the back of his neck. "I'll undo the straps," Mitch said, "But remember, I'll have this at your head the whole time."

"The WHOLE time? Aww, c'mon, Mitch, if you wanna look then just ask. I would've thought we were beyond the whole size issue at our age but hey, you're the boss. I'm not exactly in a position to argue."

Mitch pressed the gun a little harder into Matt's head, then gave up and undid the straps. Matt grinned at him as he worked on the buckles. "Want me to hold the gun? You'd be able to work faster with two hands."

Mitch made some comment under his breath and then stood back, gesturing for Matt to walk in front of him. They made their way to the small downstairs toilet with Matt talking incessantly about anything that came into his head. By the time they stepped back into the room Mitch's face was glowing with rage and the small space looked even smaller due to the crowd that waited for them.

Blade, Sean, Grace and two other men had arranged themselves around the chair. They made no comment but glowered as Matt sat down again. He smiled at Grace. "Nice to see you again, M'am. I'd offer you a seat but…well, there are none. Sorry!"

Mitch strapped him down again forcefully, almost ripping the straps in the process. Grace fired him a look as he took his place beside her, elbowing Blade out of the way. Mitch steadfastly ignored her, scowling at Matt instead. Finally Grace stepped forward and took Matt's chin in her hand, twisting his face up to look at her.

"What are we going to do with you, Mr Carter?" she said wistfully.

He managed to grin at her. "I think we're past the formal stage, Grace. Please call me Matt."

Grace smiled coldly. She let go of Matt's chin and cocked her head. "What would you do in our situation?"

Matt frowned for a moment, pretending to think. His heart was hammering in his chest and he focused on controlling his breathing. Finally he smiled up at her. "See, I should say something cute like, "Send me home to my Momma with a note about my bad behaviour" or maybe "Let me off with a warning" but to be honest…," he sighed and shrugged. "What I would really do is either wound me so I couldn't overpower your pathetic guards and get away by myself, you know what I mean? Go for the good wound. Or maybe I would kick the shit out of me just to make you all feel netter, take a few photos and send them to Shannon and my Dad with a ransom demand or whatever kind of demand you people are intending to make. How am I doing?" He sighed theatrically. "It's been a while y'know? I'm out of practice with this shit. Hear anything you like the sound of yet?"

Blade swore. "Smart mouthed American asshole. Maybe if we cut your tongue out you wouldn't sound so defiant." He moved forward, sliding a thin knife from inside his shirt and pressing it against Matt's neck. Matt managed to keep his body motionless and Grace made a noise somewhere between amusement and exasperation. She laid a hand on Blade's shoulder and, after a few moments of staring into Matt's eyes, he moved back into line.

Grace turned her attention back to Matt. "As you can see, Mr Carter, not everyone here thinks that keeping you in your current pristine state is a good idea. We did, however, come up with a compromise." She smiled at him again, showing teeth and glanced briefly at the others in the room who, Matt supposed, were also smiling now. He didn't check that particular theory out, keeping his attention on Grace. She gave a brief nod and the two balaclava-clad strangers on Sean's right brought their hands from behind their backs, revealing large baseball bats. "We thought it was appropriate." Grace smiled again and Matt sighed.

"So, your guys get to have some fun and you get to blackmail my Dad," Matt said, barely managing to keep the shake out of his voice.

There was obviously nothing left for Grace to say to him. She gave orders to Mitch to "Lose the chair, I don't want it in shot," and to the rest of the thugs, "Beat him about a bit but don't kill him. He has to be left alive." Satisfied that everything was as she wanted it and that Sean had remembered to put a memory card in the camcorder, Grace left without a backward glance.

The door was barely closed before they started.

The first man went for Matt's stomach and, as he doubled up, the air whooshing out of his lungs, the second went for his legs. The noise was as loud as a gunshot in the small room. Thwack! Matt felt something pop in his knee and the world fragmented into a billion pinpricks of light. He went down hard, trying to curl into a ball as his shoulder took a shot, the backs of his legs, the small of his back. He grunted with every contact, little explosions of pain lighting up all over his body. There was blood under him; the men's shoes were sliding in it. He could smell it and taste it. He wanted to retch, wanted to drift away.

Mitch stepped in and turned him over, his face impassive. The two men moved in again, Sean zoomed in with the camera; Matt braced himself as best he could and then Mitch's phone rang.

For a few seconds all action ceased and the men above him looked at each other comically. Mitch rolled his eyes and pulled the phone from his jeans, he checked the caller display and his face turned ashen.

With a weirdly accurate flash of intuition, Matt knew exactly who was on the line. He managed to grin.

****

"If your boys hit him one more time I'll kill you all," Shannon hissed into Mitch's ear. He didn't ask how she knew what they were doing, just glanced down at Matt. The bastard was actually grinning at him through a mouthful of blood.

He glanced around at the others and managed to pull himself together. "Really? And how will you manage that, sweetheart?" Mitch puffed out his chest and pasted a smug smile on his face. The others in the room relaxed.

Shannon's voice was calm and steady. "Hit him again and you'll find out." she said.

Mitch frowned and thought for a moment. There was silence in the room and the tension notched up again. "Put the bats down." he said finally. The two men looked at each other and one of them pulled up his balaclava. He was blond and baby-faced, no more than seventeen or eighteen. He opened his mouth to speak, took in Mitch's glower and shrugged. "For fuck sake put them down!" Mitch bellowed and waited until it was done.

"Now what?" he asked into the phone, turning away from the men's confused looks and Blade's sneer. He couldn't face his son – Sean would have a look of disappointment on his face. Mitch felt a stab of self-loathing and pressed his lips together until they stung.

"Now you get the organ grinder on the phone. I'm sick of talking to the monkey." Shannon was still talking calmly but Mitch heard the steel in her voice. He opened his mouth to argue, to call her a name, he wasn't sure what but she spoke again before he did. "Just get Grace, Mitch. Stop pissing around and trying to act the big man. Everyone in that room knows who and what you are now."

Mitch turned to Sean. His shoulders felt heavy and he was getting a headache. "Get your Mother," he rasped.

"What? But…" Sean began.

"Now, damn you! NOW!"

Mitch watched his son march from the room and turned his attention to the others. Blade was the only one looking him in the eye with an expression of gleeful satisfaction. Mitch wanted to kill him. He had a feeling that his son would never look him in the eye again.

On the floor Matt moaned and managed to roll onto his side into a foetal position. He didn't know what was going on but he wished they'd hurry up. Every inch of his body from the neck down was either on fire or numb. His mind was starting to have problems coping with all the pain and the delayed shock. It wanted to shut down for a while and he wanted to let it but he knew that he had to stay awake. He tried to concentrate on relaxing each of his limbs in rotation but he kept drifting away. Without realising it he drifted into unconsciousness and, above him, no-one noticed.

Grace walked into the room, her face like thunder. With a glare at Mitch she snatched the phone from him and spoke slowly and carefully into it. "Alright then, Shannon, I'm Grace. What can I do for you?"

****

Matt woke with a thumping headache. He moved slightly to clear his blurred vision and an avalanche of pain flared through his body. He moaned and swam through a swamp of inky blackness for a while. When he came to again, Erin was beside him.

"Here, Matt, drink this." Her voice seemed to come from far away and then close by, like moving through radio frequencies. She tenderly lifted his head and inserted a straw into his mouth. The cool water tasted like nectar and Matt took several sips, feeling it slide down his parched throat and into an empty stomach. Erin pulled the straw away before he could take too much and gently laid his head back down on to the thick pillows.

"Where am I?" Matt asked, his voice thick and ragged.

Erin busied herself with some task outside of his field of vision. "You're still in the house in Portstewart. Downstairs bedroom. You've been out of it for almost two days. I was beginning to think you'd never bloody wake up but the fever's subsiding and you've a better colour about you."

Matt carefully turned his head towards her voice, grimacing at the pain each movement brought and also at the syringe in her hand.

"What is it?" He asked.

Erin concentrated for a moment, injecting a small amount of a clear fluid into his arm. "It's okay. It's just a strong pain killer. You have a few broken bones – definitely two in your right leg, one in your right arm, possibly a rib or two and your shoulder was dislocated."

"Was?"

"I reset it." She caught his look and shrugged. "I was a nurse. I've done what I could but, well, you really need proper medical attention and everyone's a bit too wired just now for me to start asking for any more than I've been given."

Matt frowned as he mentally assessed his injuries. Now that he was concentrating on them, he could feel the tight bandages and the liquid hot pains which rose above the others. His memory came back with a bang.

"They wanted to kill me." he said, his voice flat with certainty. "Shannon? She called them?"

"Relax, Matt." Erin sat down beside him, careful to avoid

nudging him. Shannon phoned as they were pounding on you and, well, I don't know the whole story, I just caught bits and bobs, but apparently she made some threat, spoke to Grace and brokered a deal. Grace has been thumping around like a woman possessed ever since."

"A deal? What kind of deal? What's Mitch's opinion?"

Erin shrugged again. "He's been very quiet on it and like I said, I don't know much. Blade's involved, you're involved and midnight on Thursday…um, tomorrow now I suppose, well, that's the time. Beyond that? Dunno."

Matt was frowning. His brain couldn't seem to focus on one thing at a time. For Shannon to make a deal was odd, for Grace to go along with it was even more confusing. And Blade? So many pieces of the puzzle and his brain was just too fuzzy to sort them out and slot them into place. He looked at Erin – another puzzle piece. "You've helped me," he said gently. "Why?"

"I promised I would," she told him. She walked to the window and ran a hand through her hair. "I love Sean. That doesn't mean that I agree with what he does for a living. I've always turned a blind eye to all that shite but, well, it's all got so…"

"Close to home?" Matt asked.

She grimaced. 'It was always close to home, Matt. I just managed to pretend it wasn't but now I need some stability. I need a proper home; I need my husband around and not off playing terrorist. I need somewhere safe to raise my baby." She turned to face Matt and her eyes were full of tears.

Matt sighed and held out his hand to her, ignoring the furnace of pain in his shoulder. Erin looked at it for a moment, then walked over and allowed him to take her small white hand in his.

"How long have you known?" asked Matt.

She grinned shyly, "Not long, I'll be twelve weeks on Sunday so it's early days yet."

"Well, congratulations, Erin. If your nursing skills are anything to go by then you'll make a terrific Mom. Is Sean pleased?" Erin gently pulled her hand away and walked slowly back to the window. Matt drew in a breath. "He doesn't know?"

"No," he voice was barely a whisper. "It never seemed to be the right time to tell him." Erin buried her face in her hands and sobbed. Matt watched her. He couldn't think of anything to say, any way to make her feel better. His heart wanted to tell her that everything would be ok but his brain was telling him to shut up. Apart from anything else, he couldn't trust anyone in this house.

Erin whirled around suddenly and threw herself down beside his bed. "He'll be killed," she sobbed. "What can I do?"

Matt wrestled with his conscience. He wanted to help her but he needed to protect his own back, and perhaps Shannon's too. He shook his head, trying to clear some of the fog and then he touched her head with his fingertips.

"I want to help you, Erin, but I don't have enough information. If I knew what the plan for tomorrow night was then I could maybe work out a way to keep you and Sean safe." He paused. She was looking at him with a kind of helpless optimism. He forced himself to go on. "Can you help?"

She blinked, thought for a moment and then slowly shook her head. "I don't know. They don't trust me much." She looked him in the eye. "Like you don't trust me." She saw his face and gave him a sad little smile. "I understand, Matt. I really do. I've been around people who trust nothing and no-one since the day I was born. You're a survivor and you've learned to be cautious." She stood up and smoothed down her skirt. "I'll try. For Sean and me, for our baby. I'll see what I can find out."

Matt lay still for a long time after she left. His mind drifted, sorting through various options and scenarios. He had no idea what arrangements had been made, what deal had been brokered but whatever happened, people were going to die. Just before he fell asleep he realised that he didn't want to die yet and that he would help Erin and Sean if he could. He knew what it was like to be born into a family with a history and expectations. He also knew that getting out of those obligations was damn near impossible.

He was living proof.

Chapter Twenty-five

Thursday morning dawned bright and cold. Autumn was well under way but summer was finding it hard to let go. The sun and moon fought for supremacy in the early morning sky but the leaves were falling from the trees around the army base.

The small team made their way from Ballykelly in the borrowed contractor's van without speaking. Everyone was concentrating on the part that they had to play in the day's operation. Shannon was glad of the silence. She felt tense and relieved all at the same time. By this time tomorrow she would have revenge for her family but she felt it in her gut that not all of the men sitting around her would survive. She watched them all from the corner of her eye. There were eight of them altogether. From what Denton Fraser had said they came from several agencies but they seemed to gel well together. She was acutely aware of their controlled tension and the way that they had treated her since the briefing yesterday – at first there had been unease, then a grudging acceptance, respect and now? It was like being on a day trip with eight older brothers. She shivered. They could die today. How would she feel if her plan ended with their deaths? Shannon shook herself and clambered over the seat into the cab.

The one called Frank was driving again, still wearing his ridiculous shades. She wondered if he ever took them off and had a vision of him climbing into bed dressed in blue and white striped pyjamas and his sunglasses. She smiled.

"Somethin' funny?" Frank asked, unsmiling, in a bland monotone. Shannon cocked her head at him, she had the strangest feeling that they had met before, something in his voice triggering a memory.

"Weird, isn't it?" she said, leaning her elbow on the window rest.

"Is it?" Frank kept his eyes on the road, his enquiry neutral.

"Yeah. Yesterday I thought you were the most bland and boring guy I'd ever met but today? Today you're actually growing on me. Today I find you sexy, devilishly handsome. There's this animal attraction between us. You can't deny it."

There was a muffled chuckle from the back of the truck. Shannon was careful not to smile.

Frank sighed disdainfully. "You have a very weird sense of humour, M'am." He turned to look at her and his lips curved up slowly into a grin. Shannon grinned back. They passed a signpost for Portstewart and the smile slipped from her face. "You okay?" Frank was looking back at the road but his dreary couldn't-give-a-shit tone was gone, replaced by a note of concern.

"Honestly?"

Frank nodded.

"I'll be glad to get this over with. I know you…we…can get Matt back. I know we can get the cell, all of them. I just worry about our casualties."

Frank chewed that over for a moment. "This is what we do, Shannon. Wherever we go, whatever the job is, whoever we're with, we know there's a chance we might not be coming back. If that's something we can't deal with, then we're in the wrong job. Lewis Carter brought us together because he believes we can handle ourselves, no matter how nasty the situation gets." He jabbed his thumb towards the back of the van. "Those guys in there may come from different companies, different agencies but they're professionals, same as the team already dug in around the crescent. We all know the risks. You just deal with your part in this – it's a team effort remember. Soon as you start worrying about the others in the team, that's when things start to go fubar. You keep yourself safe and don't worry about us. We can take care of ourselves."

Shannon sat studying Frank for a moment. "What?" he said.

"Fubar?"

"Yeah, fubar."

"Frank that's a rubbish word. You made it up."

Frank scowled at her. "Didn't you ever watch 'Saving Private Ryan'?"

"No," Shannon was smiling.

Frank shook his head. "Gentlemen," he shouted into the back

of the van. "Care to tell the lady what 'fubar' means?"

They answered in unison. "Fucked up beyond all recognition, M'am."

Shannon sat back in her seat, laughing. The road signs were giving Portstewart as being twenty-three miles away now. She sucked in a breath and released it slowly. A little under twelve hours to go.

Chapter Twenty-six

Matt lifted his head and resisted the urge to just close his eyes and drift off to sleep again. They had moved him back into the living room and, with difficulty, back into the wheelchair. He thought he might have screamed at some point. The pain had been so bad. He knew he had a slight fever and several broken bones but he was also having some problems with his vision from time to time. He couldn't figure out if his vision kept blurring because of the fever, the medication that Erin had been liberally dosing him with or if the beating in the white room had something to do with it. Something to do with it? He grinned at his own train of thought. That beating had something to do with every pain in his body right now.

According to Erin, today was Thursday and whatever they were here to accomplish would go down tonight. And 'here' had been a surprise.

The house that they were in now was directly across the bay from Shannon's. Just in front of it were the harbour and the small car-park where he had watched for her coming home from her run. It felt like years ago that he had sat out there on the hood of the borrowed car and swallowed pain killers with cold coffee before setting off to perform his duty for his dear old dad.

They had kept him in the living room at the front of the house behind a set of vertical blinds which were tilted to keep nosy parkers from looking in and seeing him, but gave him a perfect view of where he was.

Once he'd recognised their location he'd begun running possible scenarios through his head – what would he do if he was Mitch Connor? Or was it Grace who was making these decisions? He was betting on Grace. Coming back to Portstewart wasn't something that Mitch would've done. It was too obvious for a start and Shannon knew the place too well. Of course there were no guarantees that she would come back here at all but Matt knew that she would – this was the point of it all, to take this group down. All of them.

She'd made some kind of deal with Grace and Matt was betting it was an exchange – she'd give herself to them in return for his release. Just what they wanted, what Grace had planned. What Matt had to figure out was if Shannon was actually planning on going through with it or if she'd made it to some help.

Today he'd had his answer.

First of all the road to Shannon's house had been closed off right outside the town hall. An inflated road crew in fluorescent jackets had begun digging up a section of the road causing traffic chaos and all kinds of arm waving and rude gestures from the locals. Matt had fallen asleep around eleven and woken again after one. Immediately his eyes had fallen on the changes in the tableau before him. The fluorescent brigade had gone and, although the road was still closed, 2 large vans emblazoned with the colours of a local haulage company had been allowed through. Matt counted twelve men carrying various items of furniture into one of the vans.

Mitch was sitting on one of the concrete bollards at the harbour watching the comings and goings with interest. As Matt watched he smoked three cigarettes in a row, lighting one off the other and then turned and came back into the house. Matt caught his look as he climbed the steps but looked away. He had nothing left to say to Mitch Cooper, Michael Connor, or whatever the traitorous git wanted to call himself.

Matt returned his attention to Shannon's house. The removal men were packing up and making a big deal about closing up the house and locking the back of their van. Matt grinned. Only four men got back into each van. The other four had disappeared. If he's had to put money on it, he would've bet they were holed up in the house. He wondered if Mitch had noticed.

Both vans moved away, made their way past the road closure and were soon up the hill past the Church of Ireland and out of sight. For the next hour there was no movement either around Shannon's house or the house he was in so Matt allowed himself to fall asleep again.

He awoke just after sunset and the house was filled with noises and smells. He closed his eyes and tried to concentrate on the pictures his other senses could paint for him.

Somewhere at the rear of the property, Grace was giving orders. The actual words escaped him but he got the general idea that things weren't proceeding fast enough for her liking and she was biting off the head of anyone who got close enough. Blade's gravelly drawl responded to her with a furious torrent, his closing words punctuated with the slamming of a door.

The smells bothered him. Apart from the usual cooking smells that all houses have from time to time (mainly toast today, slightly burnt) and the strong aroma of polish and old leather from his room there was another. The more Matt strove to distinguish it from the rest of the aromas reaching him, the more certain he became of what it was. It took him back to a myriad of nights spent in the comforting ritual of cleaning his guns, loading and reloading, checking the action of each individual component. Nights spent looking after the very things that would keep him alive. He inhaled deeply and sighed. He smelt gun oil. And lots of it. Matt realised that he was suddenly breathing hard. He was thinking about Shannon, wondering if she knew that Grace might be willing to kill her. He rolled his eyes, banging his head on the back of the chair in frustration. He was tied down, so he wouldn't be much help to her when (if?) she came. He grimaced. Even if the straps were undone he wouldn't be able to walk, Mitch and his heavies had rendered him useless. And perhaps that had been the plan. Suppose this was all part of the plan? Suppose they knew that he was good bait? That Shannon was relying on Lewis Carter for help? That Shannon would have no choice but to come and get him? They had made sure that he would be of no help to a rescue party and getting him out would be doubly difficult.

He pulled his gaze back to the now dark shape of Shannon's house, willing her to be one step ahead of Mitch and Grace this time. Frustration boiled over and he beat his fist against the arm of the wheelchair.

He tensed as the door to his room opened softly behind him. Erin knelt down beside him and, for a few seconds, she said nothing. Simply stared out across the bay. Matt turned in the chair to look at her – she was dressed in a pair of black leggings and a black t-shirt. Her hair was tied back in a severe pony tail and her face was pale and worn.

"I'm to go with them," she said softly, keeping her eyes firmly fixed on the window. Matt saw a tear slide down her cheek. He twisted his hand around in the strap and held it open. She smiled sadly and placed her hand in his, drawing some comfort from the contact.

"Have you ever…?" Matt couldn't think of a delicate way to ask. Erin saved him the trouble.

"Gone with them before? Used a gun? Killed another human being? Dressed in skanky black leggings and hunted someone down? No to all of the above. It's like something you'd see at the pictures."

"Pictures?"

Erin looked at him. "Movies. I keep forgetting you're a bloody yank. I was always just the bait 'cause I look kinda unthreatening. And they never taught me to fight or fire a gun 'cause they knew I'd be shite at it."

Matt tilted his head in one side. His senses were screaming at him. He wanted to advise this sad, scared girl. He wanted to hold his tongue and get out of this alive. He wanted to help her. He couldn't trust her. He wanted to trust her. If he was going to do something to help her then he had to do it now. Time was running out for both of them.

"Erin," he began, "I'm willing to bet that there are a lot of guns in this house tonight. And that means that there's going to be a lot of gunfire later." He gripped her hand tight. "I know that you don't want to be a part of this. You want your family to be far away, to be safe. Take my advice, honey. For what it's worth – get yourself lost in the dark before all the shit starts. Persuade Sean to go with you. Tell him about the baby. Give him the chance to come with you and if he doesn't then you just turn around and start running. Don't stop until you and your baby are safe. I lost my family, Erin. They were killed by a terrorist cell that was targeting me. Maybe if someone had told me before, maybe I could've saved them. I've spent so long mourning my wife and my daughter." He took a breath to steady his voice. "You don't have your family yet but even the loss of the dream of them would be as bad as losing real flesh and blood." He paused. "Do you get this? I'm not real good as talking about this shit."

Erin's lips were trembling and her chin was wobbling. She stood up and gently embraced Matt. He could feel her heart beating wildly against his, tasted the salt of her tears as she touched her lips to his and then she backed away from him, mouthing 'thank you' as she went. The clock struck the hour and he counted them. Ten o'clock. It was going to be a long night.

Chapter Twenty-seven

They were lying against the rocks, all four of them silent and motionless. The stone dug into their skin through their clothes and yet none of them had moved in almost an hour.

The hill behind Grace's house was an even better vantage point than Shannon had hoped. It rose almost sixty feet above the harbour, right behind the large three storey houses. The top of the hill was flat with a car park and coast guard look out, both deserted tonight. Beyond that and to their right the ocean stretched out across the horizon. Shannon licked her lips and could taste the salt. She felt a pang of homesickness.

From her position on the rocky slope of the hill she could look down on the back of Grace's house and beyond it, across the bay, to her own. Earlier this afternoon, after gathering up a few possessions, she had stood for a few minutes in the calm and quiet of her living room enjoying the view. She knew it was the last time. She could never come back. It hurt worse than she had expected and the hurt fuelled a well of dark anger that had been simmering for years. Lying out here in the dark for the past hour, her thoughts had been of her mother, her father, her sister, her brother, Matt. and then of Blade, Mitch, Grace, Sean, Erin. She saw Mitch's face most of all, heard his lies again and felt the punch of his betrayal in her gut over and over. The anger lay coiled inside of her, waiting to be released.

Shannon checked her watch and signalled for a pair of night goggles. They were passed up the line swiftly and silently. She lined them up and focused them on Grace's back yard. It was well patrolled. Three men around the perimeter, walking back and forth, two inside the enclosed yard and probably another just inside the back door. It was as they were expecting. So far so good. She passed the goggles back. Midnight was approaching and she was expecting them to make their move before that.

A voice whispered in her ear piece. "Echo one, this is echo two. Movement to the front. Three men, one woman, heading up and onto the lower prom. No weapons in plain sight. I repeat no weapons in plain sight."

Shannon touched the connector at her throat and spoke softly. "This is echo one. We have five definites and one possible at the back. Base can you confirm that the other houses are empty?"

There was a pause and then Lewis Carter's voice came through. "Confirmed echo one. Target is the only inhabited premises." He paused and there was a smile in his voice when he spoke again. "There's an election coming up and we canvassed for a local candidate. Connor was full of info. Told us the other houses were holiday homes. We tried them anyway but there's no-one home. Base out."

Shannon glance swept towards her old home once again and she froze. She motioned for the goggles again and focused on the speck that she could see on the dark water. Cursing she opened contact again. "Echo three. We have a boat in the water, heading for your position."

"I have it echo one. Do we engage?"

"Only if you have to, echo three. We want to hold your position as long as possible. Keep me informed."

"Understood, echo one. Holding position. Echo three out."

The agent beside her gave her a nudge and signalled below them. Shannon swung the goggles back to the house. The back door was open and three of the men from the patrol were standing there, talking animatedly. One disappeared for a moment and came back with cigarettes and a lighter. Shannon grinned. "Don't ya know nicotine'll kill ya?" she whispered to herself. She checked the other patrol. Three men, still on the perimeter. It was now or never.

Taking a deep breath, she signalled to Agent Alan Harris. He slithered forward to sit next to her. She opened the intercom link so that everyone would know what was happening. "Three inside the back door, smoking. Three on the perimeter. Take the perimeter out. You need to be quick, it's a triangle formation so if one sees the other go down we're fubar."

Harris grinned and pulled his rifle up beside him. Shannon

pulled back to give him room. He slid forward a fraction, pulled the scope around and settled himself. Shannon held her breath as Harris swung the weapon in a gentle arc, sighting the three men. It was tight; he wouldn't have much time to line up all the shots. He watched for a few seconds, his large frame still and quiet. Then he took out the man patrolling the left side of the line of houses. The silenced shot made a low oomph sound but the target fell silently, then Harris swung to the right and took out the second, just as he approached the corner where the first man lay. The third was down several seconds later as he rounded the East corner. Shannon exhaled, patted Harris on the shoulder and motioned the others forward.

The climb down took less than a minute but Shannon's heart thumped with frustrated adrenaline until they reached the ground. If they were caught outside the house, the whole operation was over. The longer they were on the rocks, the more vulnerable they became.

Shannon's radio hissed. "Echo one, this echo three. We have changed position. We are around twenty feet east of our previous. Boat has anchored off shore and we have company. I count four men currently bedding in just under the house to the west of our current. Echo three out."

Shannon frowned. "I have that echo three. Hold position unless you are compromised." She squinted into the house, trying to see around the corners that separated her from the rest of the team.

"Echo one." That was Lewis.

"Receiving, base." Shannon waited.

"Echo four in position awaiting your orders. Base out."

"I have that base." She paused. "Check in echo four."

Another hiss of static. "Echo four receiving. We are in position and ready to rumble. Echo four out."

Shannon grinned. "Glad to give you something to do on a Thursday night, echo four. Stay ready. Echo one out."

Frank appeared, silhouetted against the kitchen door. He beckoned them forward. Shannon froze. This was off the script.

Beside her, Harris frowned. The signal was three bursts on the com when it was clear to come in. Shannon looked at Harris, gave him a nod and he moved into the shadows of the yard, heading for the large kitchen window.

Shannon waited until Harris was in position just to the right of the window and then she moved cautiously forward. Frank hadn't moved. He was looking in her general direction with that lazy couldn't-care-less way that he had. She studied his face as she moved. His gaze was unwavering. She moved out of the shadow of the wall for a second and his eyes widened. She moved back and waited. His eyes were fixed on her now. He blinked once and lifted his head a fraction. Shannon opened her radio. "Echo one to all units. We are entering a PT1 situation here. Stay alert. I'm keeping you ITL. One out."

Shannon caught the ghost of a smile cross Franks' face. PT1 was agent slang for a possible trap. ITL meant 'In the Loop', which meant that she was leaving her coms open so that they would be able to hear what was happening. She glanced towards Harris. He was raising his rifle, all his attention became focused between the crosshairs. She moved quickly forward, out of the shadows and into the doorway for a split second. There was movement behind Frank and she dived to the ground.

There were two shots. One just skimmed above her head and the other came from Harris. It was the same dull oomph as before, followed this time by a soft, wet slap and a thud. Frank moved quickly, grabbing a small semi-automatic from the ground and disabling it. He threw it back into the yard as Shannon dusted herself off and moved alongside him.

"How many?" She asked.

Frank was checking his own gun. "The three that we know about, another two on the ground floor and I would hazard a guess that the other two floors will have at least two each. Minus this guy," he gestured towards the slumped form inside the door. "I make that eight to bring down."

Shannon nodded. "Closing coms. Location checks please." She pulled off her black wool hat and shook her hair free. They were in. She could make a start on her part of the operation.

The rest of the team called in their positions in rotation.

"Echo two in position. Trio in transit. Two out."

"Echo three covering targets on the rocks. Looks like it's a WW until they move. Three out." Shannon raised an eyebrow.

"WW is 'Watch and Wait,'" Frank told her. "Dammit, woman, you were doing so well out there with the lingo."

"Echo four picking up trio, folding back and into the house. Four out."

Shannon checked her watch. "This is echo one. All received. We are now on a stiff clock, gentlemen. I make it 12:16. Once the trio is at the house, our time is up. At best we have ten minutes to locate the target, round up the cell and close these bastards down. Let's not waste time. Echo four – keep them alive, they're the principals. Echo three – give us five minutes and then detain at will. Take them earlier if they make a move. Echo two – once they get inside, it's up to you to seal all exits. Sound off and…and… good luck." She paused. "Echo one out."

"Echo two locked and loaded. Two out."

"Echo three ready to kick ass. Three out."

"Echo four live and dangerous. Four out."

"Base to Echo one. Shannon, I …Rebecca…." Lewis Carter's voice was cracking. He wanted to say so many things – look after my boy, take care in there, stay alive – but he was Lewis Carter, there was a reputation to uphold and a group of men with their lives on the line for his operation. They didn't need an over the hill soft politician. "Show them who they're messing with." he rasped, his voice hissing through the com static. "Base out."

Shannon clicked off her radio and moved inside after Frank and Harris. They were moving at speed now, the clock was ticking down.

They'd been over the drill so many times in the past two days that it was now second nature. At the stairs, Frank and Harris moved on up, leaving Shannon to take care of the ground floor. Frank looked back once, caught her eye for a split second and opened his mouth to say something. Shannon grinned at him.

"I know who you are," she mouthed. He nodded and was gone. Shannon pulled the heavy revolver from her hip, grasped it in both hands and moved down the hall, swinging it in front of her in a wide arc. She knew the layout by heart so the doors held no surprises, only possibilities. She checked each room. They were empty. And then there was only one left. The living room.

Shannon paused at the door, listening intently. They knew by now that someone was coming. They would have heard her in the other rooms. If Frank was right then there were two of them. If she was right, then Matt was in this room too.

She stayed to the left of the door, raised the gun to shoulder height and took a deep breath before making her entry. Then she froze, released the breath and lowered the gun. All her senses were alive and tingling. The very air around her felt heavy and thick, resonating with energy. Slowly she turned to face the wall. Closing her eyes, she transferred the gun to her left hand, stretched out her right and pressed the palm against the door.

Upstairs there was a shout, a blast of gunfire, the sound of running.

Shannon tuned it all out and concentrated on the feeling of the warm wood beneath her hand, the waves of energy flowed around her and she allowed her mind to reach out. The picture came clearly into her mind. Grace had not kept her word. Blade had not gone to the house with her: he was here, in this room, holding a knife to Matt's throat. Holding it so close that a thin line of blood had begun to seep around it.

Shannon was suddenly relaxed. She was breathing deep, regular breaths. She concentrated on blocking out Matt's distress, anger, fear. She took in the rest of the room – the picture window, the book shelves, the old leather suite; the man crouched behind the door, the straps on the wheelchair biting into Matt's arms. She returned her attention to Blade. He was wound up, ready for action. She could feel his disgust, could even see the anger on his face. Matt took a slow breath and she felt him calm and centre his attention on the door. They knew someone was out there.

Shannon took her hand from the door and bent her head,

biting her lip. If she played this wrong Matt would die and so would she. She turned slowly around again, putting her back to the wall and slid down. The second target was on the right hand side of the door, crouched low just like she was. She counted to three.

"Blade," she whispered.

Chapter Twenty-eight

Blade shuddered.

His eyes darted around the room, into the deep shadows on either side of the window, down low by the door where one of Grace's lieutenants, a quiet big man by the name of Murphy, was crouched. Blade made a motion with his free hand and Murphy looked up. They glared at each other.

Blade motioned for him to come over and, shaking his head, he rose soundlessly to his feet and made his way back across the room.

"What?" Blade asked in a low whisper.

Murphy blinked. "You called me over, what do you want?"

Blade rolled his eyes. "You whispered my name ya prat."

"No, I didn't. Everything was quiet and then you signalled for me to come over here." The man spread his hands out wide. "I hadn't spoken until you did."

They glared at each other some more.

Matt chuckled softly and Blade swung around in front of him. "Somethin' funny, dead man?"

Matt smiled at him. "You're an idiot."

Blade swung a fist at Matt's head, taking the knife away from his throat as he moved. The blow caught him on the side of the head and it was a hard punch, knocking him and the wheelchair sideways. He hit the ground with a thud and Blade was moving in, his namesake in his left hand to finish the job when the voice echoed around the room. "Blade," it whispered over and over.

Blade turned astonished eyes to the man beside him. "You hear that, right?" Murphy nodded mutely, glancing around with wide eyes. Blade's own eyes narrowed. "It's that witch, she's here for me. Well, if she thinks she can put one over on me then she has a trick or two still to learn. Hear that, bitch?" His voice rose. "Come and get me, then. You'll end up with my knife in your gut, just like your brother."

The voice stopped and Blade grinned. "Yeah, thought that

might get your attention. You want to know how he died? I set him loose in Toorleitra Woods, gave him a five minute head start and then hunted him down and gutted him like a fish. He lived for a while after that, screamin' and squirmin' and callin' for his mammy." Blade chuckled and scratched the stubble on the side of his face with the flat of his knife. Matt shuddered and closed his eyes. The man was insane. He opened his eyes again and realised that the shadows in the room seemed to have lengthened. And was it colder? His breath fogged in front of his face. Blade was still cackling and murmuring about good times and fresh kills and young flesh. Murphy had gone completely still; he was watching the door with intense concentration.

Matt followed his gaze. Was the handle turning? He blinked and tried to squint into the gloom, turning his head a little to get a better view. Pain stabbed into his temples again and he moaned. Blade's attention swung back to him. "Awww, poor fella. Is your wee head sore?" He leaned over and grinned at Matt. "I'll see your blood spilled before I leave this room," he whispered.

"You first," said Shannon and her gun barked twice. Blade's mouth dropped open in astonishment even as his body dropped to the floor beside Murphy's. A matter of seconds and both men were dead. Matt tried to focus. Shannon seemed to be made of smoke, her body becoming more solid as he watched. He almost put it down to hallucinations caused by the pain killers but memories of the day in Ballystewart made him rethink.

Shannon knelt down beside him and Matt grinned at her, wincing. "Quite an entrance."

She grinned, her eyes flicking towards Blade. "Didn't think I'd get any second chances. Where are you hurt?" She was carefully undoing the wheelchair straps.

"Everywhere," Matt groaned. "At least that's how it feels."

"Can you walk?" He shook his head. "Good job they left us a wheelchair then," Shannon smiled at him but her mind was charging ahead to the others.

"Go and do what you need to, Shannon. I'll be okay." Matt flexed his wrists and struggled to pull himself into a sitting position. Shannon pushed him back.

"Quit being all macho, Carter. I already know you're a marshmallow."

He chuckled and let his head fall back to the floor. "Damn. Thought I had you fooled."

The door to the room opened with a bang, bouncing back against the far wall as wood splintered and the broken lock rolled across the floor. Shannon was rolling in front of him, gun in hand, before Matt had a chance to take a breath. Frank rushed into the room, weapon drawn, followed swiftly by Harris. They took in the scene before them and everyone relaxed. Frank raised an eyebrow at Shannon. "Take it we won't be dragging Mr Blade here back for interrogation?" He glanced at the other body. "Or his friend for that matter."

Shannon shrugged. "You can if you want but I don't think you'll get much out of either of them." She looked back at Blade's body and frowned.

Matt touched her arm. "You okay?"

She looked back at him with tired eyes. "It doesn't feel as good as I thought it would." Matt sighed and squeezed her arm..

Frank was studying the door that he'd just had to break down, a look of puzzlement on his face. He glanced at Matt, caught his eye and shrugged, letting it go. Matt released a breath he hadn't realised he was holding as Harris moved forward, checking his watch. "They should be in place by now."

Shannon nodded and spoke into her com-link. "All units, this is echo one. We have the hostage. Take the primaries. Go! Go! Go!"

She looked towards her home on the far side of the bay and saw it light up inside with muzzle-flash fireworks. Shannon closed her eyes, sank down beside Matt and took a deep breath, waiting for good news.

They didn't have long to wait, but the news wasn't all good.

****

Matt Carter woke up exactly where he expected to find himself – in a hospital bed. His mouth was dry and tasted foul but his body was floating on a magic carpet of pain killers that made him smile.

There was the low, whispered hum of conversation to his right and he slowly turned his head, seeing a kaleidoscope of colours flash across his eyes. It was incredible, like standing in the middle of a rainbow. At the far side of the rainbow, silhouetted against the window, Denton Fraser stood talking to Lewis Carter. Matt thought about calling to his father but his brain couldn't seem to connect to his voice or his mouth just yet. And that was okay. He smiled again. Everything was okay on his magic carpet inside the rainbow.

There was movement to his left and he turned to face it, enjoying another rush of colours. Maybe he was inside a bubble, he thought, not a rainbow. You'd be able to see colours reflecting off the skin of the bubble, wouldn't you?

Shannon was sitting on a chair beside the bed and watching him with an amused grin.

"I'm drugged," he wanted to tell her. "Everything's cool." His voice wouldn't comply just yet but he didn't mind, he figured she'd know about the bubble and the rainbow and the magic carpet.

She leaned forward, glancing briefly towards the window and then settling her eyes on his. "They're trying to figure it all out," she whispered. "How to explain my disappearance. The powers that be are on their way so I'm leaving as soon as you and I say goodbye. I can stay hidden for as long as I need to." She paused and closed her eyes for a moment. "Some of the good guys died, Matt. We got all the small fry but Grace, Michael, Erin and Sean made it away." She looked away for a moment, her eyes full of something dark and unsettling. Matt's bubble trembled alarmingly. He frowned and tried to concentrate on the floaty feeling but it was slipping away from him fast. He sighed, pain would come now.

Shannon leaned over and pressed a gentle kiss to his forehead. "It's weird but I'm actually going to miss you, Matt Carson." She grinned. "You're a better dancer than you think you are."

He felt himself smile as she turned to go and the dark feeling came back. Matt grabbed her hand and weakly pulled her back. He searched those grey eyes and saw the truth of her intentions there. He shook his head, frowning and angry now that his mouth and brain couldn't get their act together. She understood, though and sighed. "Yes, I'm going after them, Matt. As long as they're out there then I'm not safe, no-one is. They cut throats and plant bombs and don't care who gets hurt. I can't let that be, knowing that I could do something about it." She reached into her bag and took out a small zip-loc bag. Inside it was a blue toothbrush. Their eyes met. "I can scare the crap out of him for as long as it takes him to come out of hiding and look for me. Then I'll be ready."

Matt felt the pain come as the drugs began to wear off. He grimaced, closing his eyes. There was the soft brush of lips against his own, the sweet musk of perfume trailing across his senses and then he knew that she was gone and that he would go after her.

****

Epilogue

Three months later.

Michael Connor was sitting on the roof terrace of a house in Saravena a few hundred kilometres North-East of Bogata, smoking a French cigarette and drinking a glass of crisp Australian chardonnay. There was laughter from the house – one of his host's children was watching American cartoons, dubbed into Spanish, and her tinkling giggles carried out across the rooftops and out into the depths of the warm, velvet night.

Michael pulled his phone from his pocket and keyed in Shannon's number. He thumbed the dial button but paused. As always, he was torn between hearing her voice and staying the hell away from her. He closed the phone and grinned to himself, inhaling another lungful of smoke. He had lost everything when she turned on him. Lost his bright future as saviour of the cause, lost his son (again), his ex-wife (it was becoming a habit) and most of all he had lost her. He stubbed out the cigarette angrily and stood up, taking a walk across to the edge of the roof.

The lights of the town sparkled and Michael struggled to hold on to the smug sense of wellbeing that he'd been cultivating all day. It wasn't working. Once he started thinking about her it all got messed up again. Perhaps if he went back to Ireland? He could find Sean, get himself another new identity and live out the rest of his days hiding from Lewis Carter and his cohorts. Michael had no doubt that Carter was still looking for him – he'd participated in the torture of his son for one thing. And tried to sell his secret little bloodhound.

He pulled out his phone once more and dialled her number. Grimaced and closed it again, slipping it back into his pocket. He wondered if she was with Matt Carter right now? Were they living together? Did she lay in Matt's arms every night thinking about him? Did she ever think about him? Michael drained his glass and headed back inside. Looking back wasn't good for him anymore – it just made him maudlin. The fact was that she'd chosen Matt

Carter over him and that was that, she'd been happy to help them capture him but he'd outsmarted them that night in Portstewart and he'd outsmarted them every day since. He had a lot to be happy about.

He pulled out another cigarette and lit it, taking a deep drag. He was leaving here in the morning, taking a small plane from the local airport and hopping over the border into Venezuela to meet with an old contact. There was always someone somewhere wanting to put an end to someone else for something. It was tedious – find the target, pull the trigger, skip the country – but it was lucrative and gave him the means to stay under the Carter radar.

He was packed and ready to go so a few hours' sleep would do him good. He pulled the door to his rented room closed and didn't bother with the light. He was feeling good again, a man in control of his own destiny as always. But as he shrugged out of his t-shirt and jeans Michael felt a strange sensation – like eyes watching him from the shadows or an icy finger caressing his spine..

Michael Connor shuddered.

Note from the author:

Dear Reader,

I started writing 'Shudder' around 1990 or so and it has gone through so many drafts and changes - most memorable for me is the fact that Shannon started off running whilst listening to 'The Boss' on her 'personal cassette player' (I kid you not) and ended up with an iPod!

What never changed was the location.

I lived in Portstewart from my birth until the age of 22, and only moved a little way round the coast once I got married. I return to my favourite haunts frequently and always wished for a house at the base of the cliff below the iconic beauty of O'Hara's Castle (now Dominican College). The fact that there isn't room for a house there has made no difference to me (my imagination knows no bounds!) but it may do if you are a local and think that my 'head is going'.

I wrote most of this book sitting on Harbour Hill overlooking the harbour, the Crescent and the Promenade or from the other side of the town, parked outside the town hall waiting for my children as they attended drama classes there.

It is an absolutely beautiful town, like all of the North Coast, and I am very proud to live and work in the midst of such inspiring scenery.

If you'd like to see what Portstewart, Ballykelly, Dublin etc. are REALLY like then here are some websites to look up:

http://www.northcoastni.com
http://www.discovernorthernireland.com
http://www.visitdublin.com

Best wishes

Ashley

Acknowledgments

Big thanks to my friends Shauna, Bex, Debbie and Irene for all the reading: you guys deserve medals for having to wade through all of my horrendous grammar mistakes. Thanks also to Terry, Sofie, Tori and Hazel for taking the time to read the sixth (or maybe it was the tenth!) draft - your feedback was invaluable.

Thanks again to Nigel for the fabulous cover design (and making the book 'innards' look amazing too!) Much respect Mr. Johnston.

All my love, as always, to Katy and Jack who manage to put up with me and my weirdness without losing (all) their marbles. Mwaaaah!

Connect with me online - I'd LOVE to hear from you!

Email me: mailto:aly3008ish@gmail.com
Facebook
http://www.facebook.com/pages/Ashley-McCook/117584825012617
Twitter: http://twitter.com/@aly3008
Visit my Website: www.ashleymccook.co.uk
Read my Blog: Ashley McCook's Space